Too UNSPEAKABLE for Words

# Too
# UNSPEAKABLE
# for Words

*stories*

# Rosalind Gill

**BREAKWATER**
P.O. Box 2188, St. John's, NL, Canada, A1C 6E6
WWW.BREAKWATERBOOKS.COM

A CIP catalogue record for this book is available from Library and Archives Canada.

Copyright © 2017 Rosalind Gill
ISBN 978-1-77103-106-6

Cover illustration: *St. John's Variations IX*, by Scott Goudie

We acknowledge the support of the Canada Council for the Arts, which last year invested $153 million to bring the arts to Canadians throughout the country. We acknowledge the financial support of the Government of Canada and the Government of Newfoundland and Labrador through the Department of Business, Tourism, Culture and Rural Development for our publishing activities.
PRINTED AND BOUND IN CANADA.

Breakwater Books is committed to choosing papers and materials for our books that help to protect our environment. To this end, this book is printed on a recycled paper that is certified by the Forest Stewardship Council®.

FOR

Mom and Dad, who filled me up with stories

# CONTENTS

# TOO UNSPEAKABLE
# FOR WORDS

DAD SLAMMED HIS tea cup onto the saucer. "I won't have them Englishwomen tellin' us what to do with Nance. She's not goin' near that school. Bunch of hypocritical Anglicans. Ass-lickin' the upper class."

Mom sat back in her chair, determined. "Never mind your talk about people's rights and unions. Where does that get us? Stuck here in this little 'ouse with a crowd of rowdies for neighbours. We got to do more for our Nancy."

Dad was running out of steam. He only had so much in him. "Ah! For God's sake, Bette, don't do that to the poor child. I don't want her to grow up to be a goddamn snob from Graham's College."

But there was no winning with Mom. "I got me mind made up, Dave. And I've already paid the fee. She'll be entering Grade VII in the fall."

So Graham's it was.

It was an imposing Victorian building, with turrets and widow's walks.

On the first day of school, control and authority met me at the door. In the vestibule, hung a large print of *Boadicea the Warrior*

*Queen*, complete with helmet and impenetrable breastplate, exhorting the Britons. Then there was the acrid smell of floor polish and the sound of boards creaking under little girls' feet. Obedient little girls, all doing exactly as they were told. I was soon to learn that, in this strictly female institution, compliance with the rules was supreme. Fathers waiting for daughters inside the door stayed well behind the imaginary line. In fact, the school's message about men was that they could start being unseemly at any given time. Barring major blizzards, rowdy little brothers were simply not permitted inside.

"Come along *guerls*. Don't shilly-shally. Stand up straight."

The teachers had come all the way across the Atlantic to save us from our townie ways—no more saucy retorts, no more Irish lilt. With their cool, onion-paper skin, tweed skirts and sensible shoes, they strode around in total confidence. They knew the path forward. Graham's *guerls* were to follow suit and learn to be young ladies.

In the mornings, decked out like an English schoolgirl— blue serge tunic and jaunty beret—I ran the gauntlet down Freshwater Road, withstanding the catcalls from corner boys. "Hey ugly chops, whadda ya got under yer skirt?"

But I was a *Graham's girl* now, and above all that. We had elocution lessons, poetry readings and "deportment," like Princess Anne. Graham's was a little pocket of decorum, just off Military Road.

Before long, I was toning myself down, softening my voice and composing my gangly body, arms by my side. Willingly, I became a little daughter of the Empire, only too happy to step out of my world and into their pageantry of kings and queens, colonies, cathedrals, rose gardens, and polite little girls in buckled shoes who, curiously, seemed to think there was something special about going "to the seaside."

An ocean divided the good girls from the bad. I worked hard, desperate to bask in the security of being in the ranks of the

Too UNSPEAKABLE for Words

approved. Most of the "in" girls lived in rambling "old money" houses surrounded by lawns. After school, they played in each others' gardens, but I never got invited.

"Best not go bringing those girls back 'ere," said Mom. She kept our home spotless, scrubbed the canvas floors and hung frilly curtains in the windows. But our house was still nothing more than a shabby little post-war bungalow sitting right on the sidewalk in Rabbittown.

To be on the safe side, I made a point of avoiding the few girls from my street who had somehow made it into the school. They were definitely not of "in" girl quality and had no Graham's survival skills.

Take Georgina Butler, for example, a scruffy but plucky girl who'd been accepted into the school as a charity case. Georgina took a complete miss on the Graham's rules that everyone else (and me, for sure) followed to the last sycophantic letter:

Never display the school's name on your jacket—most uncouth. (Georgina had one with GRAHAM'S spelled out across the back in fuzzy block letters.)

Never chew gum or drop candy wrappers on the sidewalk—not even on the weekends. A teacher might see you. (Georgina sprinkled the world with Wrigley's wrappers.)

And above all:

Never call the teacher "Miss," without including her surname—that would be the height of vulgarity.

"Miss, I can't read that out loud. I stutters, Miss," Georgina would say with an existential shrug.

One day, Georgina and I ran into each other trudging our way home, up Long's Hill. She grabbed the sleeve of my blazer. "Can I come do homework at your house?" she blurted, brazen as can be, knowing full well I'd been avoiding her.

I flicked her off like a fly. "I'm not allowed to have girls over."

Before long, Georgina disappeared from the school. She was not the first girl to be deemed unsuitable, then politely but ever so firmly drummed out. In the eyes of Graham's, girls like Georgina were too unspeakable for words. Unreformable. I felt bad for not helping her. "It's no sense worrying about that Georgina," said Mom, already becoming a Graham's snob. "She never should have been admitted to the school. It turns out she's Catholic, and her Protestant mother lied on the forms to get her in."

But even Mom felt sorry for Georgina when she saw her going down the sidewalk, out of the serge tunic and back in the shiny polyester of a lesser school.

"Poor Georgina never had the mettle for Graham's."

But I had all the mettle in the world. Penmanship, spelling bees, divinity lessons, French minuet, Girl Guides, home economics, whacks on the shins with field-hockey sticks. Rule Britannia! I was game for whatever it took.

Mom was thrilled. Even joined the "Graham's Ladies Guild" and bought herself a new hat with mink trim to attend afternoon teas.

Dad mocked and snorted. "Where does your mother think she's goin' with that hat? A baywoman trying to hobnob with the merchant class. Just you remember—if you're not one of them, you'll never get in."

I, too, longed to get out of Rabbittown and live in a nicer house, on a treed street, away from the toughies. I'd wander around the tony neighbourhoods, picking out my dream home, picturing myself going to sleep in a wallpapered bedroom, upstairs under the lovely gables. Why couldn't Dad make a better life for me and Mom?

But, despite myself, I did feel sympathy for his union values—guess I had it in me. I'd think of him in school when the teachers praised some socialite for being "generous to the less fortunate." The very thing he couldn't abide: handouts to the poor.

"Bunch of thieves," he'd said when I asked him to donate to the school charity fund, "giving back a few crumbs of what they stole. Don't let that crowd make you forget who you are now, Nance. You've become a real little achiever. Anything to please those dried up old women down to Graham's. I knows now they don't think they owns the world. Well, I got news for them."

He laughed, with those raspy chuckles of his.

I knew he was right, about the teachers thinking they owned the world, but I never let on. What if anyone down to Graham's ever heard how he talked!

Thank God he never came to the school. Only Mom in her fur hat.

The report cards came home with "Excellent" and "V. Good" handwritten in black ink. I was aiming for the "deportment girdle"—the coveted blue sash awarded to "all-round girls." But it did seem strange to me that, despite all the talk of "honour" and "sincerity," some of the girls wearing the girdle were nothing more than spoiled brats who hardly made an effort at anything. And, somehow, despite my good marks and voracious desire to achieve, I was stuck in second place in my class, always behind Gillian Lancaster, a dull girl with a lisp who, despite living in a vine-covered mock Tudor mansion, didn't seem to know anything about anything, not even the Battle of Hastings. Year after year, she maintained a permanent hold on first place.

"Now then, *guerls*," said Miss Blanchard one morning in elocution class, "stand up and give an account of your Christmas dinner."

Mother of God, I thought. Let the bell ring before my turn comes. I could hardly describe the real events:

Mom had put on her Christmas apron with the mistletoe pattern and laid out the few ornaments we had: two glass angels, a shiny little Santa sleigh drawn by plastic reindeer, odd parts of a nativity scene.

Nanny was out of the seniors' home for the day. She sat on the couch, ghostly white in a flowery dress, her veiny old hands fidgeting with a candy wrapper. "Come over here, my dear," she said to me, "till I tells you how I almost died." Mom was none too pleased. Dad had done the wrong thing again. "You shouldn't 'ave your mother 'ere, frightening the poor child, Dave—she's too old and sickly."

Right after breakfast, Dad had gone into the backroom and started phoning. There was some union skirmish. Listening to the rise and fall of his murmuring through the door, I could tell he was really worried. Mom opened the door and talked over his conversation. "You'd better stop all that agitating. You're going to lose your job, next thing. And it'll be your own fault."

How I wished she wouldn't be like that. My enduring image of Mom—flooded with disappointment.

By suppertime, Dad had been chain smoking all day and couldn't control his smoker's cough. He poured himself a few fingers of rum in a juice glass and sat at the table, trying to drum up some Christmas spirit.

"How do you like what Santa brought you, Nance?" he said, as cheerfully as he could. "I managed to get the last one they had in the shop."

"Your daddy thinks the world of you," said Nan, serving herself a slice of cold turkey. "That's a grand gift."

Mom scowled at the plastic bookbag under the Christmas tree. "What were you thinking? Sure, Nancy can't turn up at Graham's with a Mickey Mouse bookbag from Woolworths!"

Dad stood up and his neck went red. "Oh, so that's all wrong too, is it? I can't even buy a present for my own daughter."

Then he picked up the bowl of cranberry sauce and fired it across the kitchen.

Mom snivelled as she got out the broom. "Go to bed now, my child. Your father's not fit to be around."


When called upon by the teacher, I stood up and told a story of a Christmas dinner I'd seen in a picture in the *Girl's Own* magazine—Mommy arriving from the kitchen with the bird on a platter, kiddies groomed and rosy-cheeked, playful puppy pulling at the white tablecloth. I stood there churning it out, as if my world revolved around such niceties. All the way through, I could hear the tinny sound of my made-up Christmas. Finally, I got to the end.

"Christmas is my favourite day," I chirped, imitating the wholesome English jolliness of the teachers.

I sat down and waited for Miss Blanchard to emit her evaluation. That's how they did it down to Graham's—if your poor mark was announced to all and sundry, you might pull your socks up, out of shame. It was character building.

"Fair," she announced, with a wry "I caught you out" look.

"Fair," which ranked below "Good" and barely above "Poor" in the marking scheme, was miles from the "Excellent" I so craved. But the Christmas ordeal was over.


Dad looked out the kitchen door, smoking, with his back to Mom.

"I knew you'd lose your job if you kept up that union nonsense," she said. "And now, with no check coming in, we won't be able to pay next term's fees down to Graham's."

He glanced back over his shoulder. "I'll find work soon. You know I haven't been well."

"Haven't been well, my eye! Getting yourself fired. Stuck in the house like a frightened puppy. I s'pose Muggins here will have to go out and get a job to pay the school fees."

And that's how Mom came to work at the Royal Stores, behind the glove counter. She'd get up early in the morning, dress in her one nice suit, then walk me to Graham's, before heading down to Water Street. Of course, I never breathed a word to the girls in my class about my mother being a clerk in a store.

After school, I'd go down there and wait for her to finish her shift. I admired her, all charm and efficiency with the customers. But, sometimes, I'd cringe for her—no matter how hard she tried to suppress her Bard's Cove accent, it rose to the surface. "The manager will 'ave to approve that refund now. 'E'll be back bye and bye."

Another sad and tender memory of Mom. Doing her best to survive in town but clinging to stories of childhood in her fabled Bard's Cove, resettled and empty of people—a place she could never go back to. "We were 'appy and wanted for nothing," she'd say. Mom's paradise lost.

When the day was over, she'd take me by the hand and we'd climb the hills to Rabbittown.

Dad would be waiting in a dark house. Since he'd lost his job, Mom was barely talking to him. He moped around from room to room and she tidied up after him, plimming the pillow on the couch where he had just been sitting.

"You're my only joy," she'd say to me. "You do well down to Graham's, my dear, and I'll be so proud."

Dad never said much to me about school—that was clearly Mom's domain, and now she was even paying the fees. But one evening, he lifted himself out of his doldrums, came into my room and looked over my shoulder at the homework I was doing. "What's that project you got there now, Nance? Looks hard."

"Never mind, Dad. You don't know what they want down to Graham's," I said. I felt guilty about pushing him away. But above all, I had to keep him out of my world of knights in shining armour.

"All right, darlin', I'll leave you to it," he said as he retreated, with a chastened look, half hurt, half amused; a look I carry with me to this day.

It was a Friday morning. I was in history class—my favourite. I knew the map of England off by heart, could trace the route of the Spanish Armada, the victorious battles of Britain. I was dreaming away, gazing at the picture of Anne Hathaway's sunny cottage that hung over the board.

The classroom door creaked open. Miss Charles rubbed her chalky hands together. "What is it, my child?"

"Could Nancy House please come to Miss Pincton's office?" said the messenger in her best elocution.

Chairs scraped as all heads turned on me.

"Dad is dead," I thought, as I rose from my chair, light-headed.

I raced down the wooden staircase. A polite tap on the head-mistress's door and into the inner sanctum, heart pounding in an echo chamber.

There sat Dad. His face looked thin and gaunt, but he was sporting a defiant little grin, holding his own in Miss Pincton's office. His overcoat was half unbuttoned and he was wearing a shirt and tie, the blue one with the partridgeberry stain Mom had not been able to get out.

Miss Pincton was standing behind her desk, in a matronly dress with a forget-me-not pattern, her large bosom protruding like a shelf.

"Your *fawtha* has come to give you a new bookbag," she said in a weary manner, focusing her eyes somewhere above the door frame.

Dad winked at me and passed me the bag. I choked out a "Thank you."

He gave me a warm smile, reached out and put his hand on my shoulder. I froze, my allegiances torn by seeing my imperfect dad sitting in the hallowed chamber of Miss Pincton's high-ceilinged office.

"You can go back to your classroom now," said Miss Pincton. Dad drew back his hand. I jumped up.

The trip back along the red runner carpet in the corridor was long. Pictures of nineteenth-century field hockey teams drifted by, the spider painted dead in his tracks on the windowsill. As I rounded the corner I heard Dad being ushered out.

"We don't like to disturb the *guerls* during school hours."

Dad coughed a few times. The big door banged shut. The sound of it went into my gut. Poor Dad had been chased away, deemed unworthy.

Now I stood there wondering what to do with the slick, red school bag that was still too cheap for Graham's. Way too cheap. I'll hide it in my locker, I thought. And I won't tell Mom. She'd be so mad.

As I rushed to the locker room, the radiator under the big window at the end of the hallway hissed and banged with an almighty thud. I looked out and saw Dad making his way through the slush down Prescott Street.

The winter sun glinted on the little bald patch on the back of his head.

# HOUSE DEVIL

"WHERE DO YOU think you're going with that lipstick on?" Nancy's mother was at the hall mirror putting on her hat. "Over to that slovenly Georgina's again!"

She waved the hatpin in the air.

"I don't know what's come over you this summer! You started the holidays in a surly sulk and now you're in full revolt. That Georgina is not fit for you. What are you doing over there all the time? You can't even stand to be in your own *'ome.*"

Nancy rolled her eyes. "Don't talk your bay talk to me, Mom. What kind of *'ome* is this? You can't even make your own *'usband 'appy.*"

Shocked by her own words, she paused for a second, then turned her saucy shoulders and headed for the door.

Her mother grabbed her by the arm. "You get right back here, my lady. I'm late for church. Now go bring that breakfast tray in to your father."

Every morning it was the same thing: a slice of bread, a piece of salt fish and a cup of tea. But the only thing that crossed his lips these days were the mood pills and the painkillers—a whole life-numbing legion of them lined up on the bedside table.

Nancy dreaded going near him. She put the tray on the bed

but he didn't stir, just lay there, eyes glazed, his rough workman's hands limp on the satin bedspread. She knew he was heavy with life, listing like a rusty old ship. She and her mother, each in her own way, had been taking detours around the empty hulk of him. But she wiped that thought.

"See you later, Dad," she said, her voice trailing off as she closed the bedroom door.

Then one last primp in the hall mirror, down the front steps and up the sidewalk, skinny white legs sticking out of red shorts.


Over at the Butlers', the blinds were still down. She knocked hard. Eventually, a sleepy-eyed Georgina emerged.

"God, Nance! Don't be bangin' the door down! We went to bed all hours last night. Me brother Jimmie turned up out of the blue from Labrador. Laid off again. Come on into the kitchen."

A few minutes later, Jimmie appeared in the kitchen doorway, barefoot and in rumpled pyjamas, with a big grin on his face. Nancy fixed her eyes on his rosy toes with their little black hairs. No one in her house ever displayed their bare feet, let alone wore pyjamas without a robe. There were gaping flaps in the pyjamas— the whole outfit seemed to hang together on a single flimsy tie just below the waist, revealing the fuzzy hairline plunging down from his belly button. He came straight over to her, so close and brazen she could smell his fausty morning breath.

He looked her up and down. "Who's that, Georgie? She's some good lookin'!"

Nancy felt the room take a spin.

Jimmie chuckled. "Better sit down girl. You look like you seen a ghost. I'm not that ugly in me jammies, am I?"


Georgina sat at the bedroom mirror, coating her eyelids with silver shadow.

"Now, don't you go gettin' a crush on Jimmie. He don't know nuttin' about goodie-two-shoes girls like you. And he's nearly twenty. Way too old."

"No he's not. Sure, I'm gonna be sixteen. And he seems real nice."

"Nice? He's the devil himself. And don't go sayin' I didn't tell ya. Now come over here till I teases your hair up. I knows how to get your mind off that Jimmie—my cousin Toughie hangs out with a buncha boys down by Signal Hill. Let's see if we can find 'em."

When they got to the hill, there were no boys to be seen. They scrambled up the pathway and flopped down on a grassy slope. Looking out over the water, the summer sea all glassy and lilac, Nancy drifted off in her mind. I'm not one bit sorry for what I said to Mom. She doesn't care about Dad.

Georgina broke in. "What do you be thinking about all the time?"

Nancy looked out to sea, at a speck of a ship making its way off Cape Spear. "There's something wrong with my father."

"Ah, he's probably okay—he's just quiet."

"No, girl. Since he lost his job, he's in bed all the time."

Nancy drifted off again, thinking about her father. In the old days, he was lively, used to play cards with her, tease her. "I gets some kick out of you, Nance," he'd say. "You're a smart one, and a real little townie. I knows you're going far in this world." Then things started going bad for him at work, and the day came when he got fired. Nancy can still remember him talking on the phone with his boss. "Don't go telling me I'm not a damn good boiler man!" he'd roared, his rage filling the little house. But when he hung up, the emotion evaporated almost immediately, dissipated like fine dust falling on the ground. After that, her father was never the same. Nancy's playful moments with him were gone.

Georgina picked a daisy and plucked the petals. "Sure, my father hasn't worked the last couple of years. Your mother got that job at the Royal Stores, what are ya worried about?"

Nancy answered slowly, like she was laying down a heavy stone. "Mom's a big fat liar. Puttin' on airs. Bragging about me going to Graham's College. I should have listened to Dad—he was right all along—they're nothing but a bunch of snobs in that school. And I turned into a real little snob myself. I wouldn't even let Dad help me with my homework."

Georgina laughed. "Graham's was way too snooty for me. But sure, Nance, you've always been the real little sook with them teachers, flouncing around in the English country dances, just like your mother wants."

"Not any more. I'm finished with Graham's." Nancy's eyes filled with rebellion. "Those teachers cheated me out of first place 'cause I'm from Rabbittown. I knows I did better than that Gillian Lancaster in the exams. She told me herself she flubbed the answers on the War of the Roses. But down to Graham's, someone like me just can't come first.

"And never mind what Mom wants. I hates her. Lying all the time, especially about Dad. 'Dave's been busy workin,'" she says to the neighbours over the fence. And then there's that old minister who comes to the house. He grew up in Bard's Cove with Mom. And that's the be-all and end-all for her. You should see how she does herself up for him, hair curled and rouge on her cheeks."

"Jeez, flirtin' with the minister! I thought my mother was bad!"

"I'm telling ya, he's always over, drinkin' her tea and eatin' her shortbread. Sometimes he even opens the middle button on his black shirt to let his belly out. It's disgusting."

Georgina's daisy was plucked down to the yellow stump. She tossed it aside and stood up. "Come on, girl. Let's go down and find the boys."


At the bottom of the hill they ran smack into them—a gang of bored Sunday afternoon teenagers looking for trouble. Georgina's cousin Toughie came right over and draped his hairy arm around Nancy's shoulders. "Wanna come out to the Battery to the bunkers with us, duckie?"

Nancy could feel a whiff of danger coming off him, but here was her opportunity to get to the bunkers, the teenage courting and cavorting spot she'd heard so much about. She looked over at Georgina, who had already hooked on to one of the other boys.

"Georgie," she called from under Toughie's arm, "do ya think we should go out there with them?"

Georgina motioned with a flick of her hand that they should definitely go along with the boys.

Toughie started scuffing down the road, pulling Nancy along. Not daring to look at his pockmarked face, she trotted beside him, her eyes focused on his boots, with the laces flying.

He's so ugly, and really rough. I should turn back.

She tried to free herself but he pulled her back with a jerk. "Don't mind me," he laughed. "I knows I got no cout' at all."

At the entrance to the bunker, Toughie clamped his hand into Nancy's groin. "I likes your curly hair—is it curly down there in your cunny too?"

Something quivered "down there." Nancy's cheeks caught fire. She turned to Georgina. "I'm not goin' in there with them. I want to go home, *now*."

But the boys pushed the girls into the bunker, blocking the entrance.

Inside, it was dank and cold and smelled of urine. Nancy held on to Georgina. "My God! Did you see what Toughie did to me? We got to get outta here."

"Don't be so foolish. Sure, Toughie got a crush on ya! What else do ya want?"

The boys teased and taunted the girls, grabbing at their arms with tobacco-stained fingers.

Within fifteen minutes, the wind in the Narrows had switched. Summer drained out of the air. Nancy shivered until her little nipples went hard under her thin T-shirt.

Toughie snickered. "Sweet Jesus! Look at her now, she's gettin' horny!"

Nancy jumped back and hit the sooty bunker wall. "Please,

let us out," she pleaded, close to tears. "I gotta go *home*."

A voice called in through the entrance. "That you in dere, Toughie?"

It was Jimmie. He looked into the bunker. "What in God's name are you two girls doin' down here?"

Nancy called to him over the boys' heads. "They've got us barred in, Jimmie."

Jimmie slapped Toughie on the shoulder. "That's enough now, Tough b'y. You got that young Nance frightened to death! Better let her go before she starts bawlin'."

One of the boys stubbed his cigarette and walked out. Game over, the rest of the pack straggled out and shuffled off. As they rounded the corner, Toughie yelled back, "Them bitches was beggin' for it."

Nancy stepped out of the bunker, none the worse for wear, just a few spots of soot on her red shorts. "Thank God you turned up, Jimmie," she gushed, placing her hand on his hard bicep. "What would we..."

But then she noticed her, a girl standing behind Jimmy, a bit of a toughie herself—large breasts bursting the buttons on her blouse, and dirty high heels with frayed tips that needed to go to the cobbler's.

"Oh! So it's Velma's turn now, is it?" said Georgina, with a snarky smile. "I s'pose you two are goin' into the bunker yourselves. Come on, Nance. Let's get out of here and let them lovebirds get on with it."


Night was setting in as the girls raced out the foggy road back to town.

"Is that really his girlfriend?" said Nancy. "He can do better than that. She's hard."

"As nails, my dear, but Jim likes a bit of hard."

Nancy looked down at her sooty shorts. "Mom would kill me if she knew what I was doin'."

"Why don't you tell her we met my cousin and she fell down

and broke her arm and we had to take her to hospital or some-thin'?" offered Georgina.

"Honest, Mom, it was raining. Georgina fell down…"

"Look at the state of you. I don't believe a word you're saying."

"We couldn't help it, she hurt her foot."

"That's not true. Coming 'ome 'ere with makeup on, smell-ing of cigarette smoke! You've been out flirting with boys."

Nancy smothered her smirk. Mom scolded and flailed her arms around, more panicked than mad. "Where's my little Graham's lady? I'm going to tell the teachers about this. You've let the school down. They'll know how to fix you and those boys."

"Who cares about that bunch of old maids! They don't know nothing about boys."

"Now, now, my child, just tell me where you've been all day. I want the real truth."

Nancy bellowed, sending a shiver through her mother's sheer curtains. "You got some nerve talking about the truth. And don't *you* be accusing *me* of flirting. I sees you with that fat ol' minister."

With that, she gave her mother an almighty shove onto the couch.

Plopped among the crocheted doilies, her mother was dazed for a second. Then she got to her feet. "I won't 'ave this behaviour in the 'ouse," she said, shaking. "Now, settle down and I'll make you your tea."

Nancy made her eyes go as hard as she could. "I don't want no tea, Mom."

The next morning, while her mother was at the clothesline, Nancy dashed over to the Butlers'. Jimmie was out on the front steps having a smoke.

"Are you all right, Nance girl?" He was all concern. "That Toughie's a young son-of-a-bitch. He didn't touch ya, did he?"

"I'm fine," she said, hands on her hips. "He's just a big bully."

"If he ever tries that again, you let me know," he said, cupping her elbow. With his touch, the blood left her head but she managed to follow him up the rickety steps and into the house.


She spent the rest of the holidays manoeuvring her way into Jimmie's company.

"You're practically living at the Butlers'," said her mother. "You must have 'em charmed to death over there—a proper Street Angel. But 'ome with us you're not fit to talk to—a proper House Devil."

"Me and Georgie are just babysittin', Ma," said Nancy, feigning innocence. "Mrs. Butler's got a lot of work on her hands with all those kids."

"I don't know what kind of a place that woman runs. I'd say she's not much of a housekeeper."

Over at the Butlers', it was, in fact, out-and-out pandemonium. No smells of bread fresh-out-of-the-oven or clean-sheets-off-the-line there. Georgina's tribe of brothers and sisters ran wild—no beds ever got made, kitchen cupboards were left open with food tumbling out, taps dripped, TV blared. Mrs. Butler spent her time in some kind of party den at the back of the house. Nancy saw people coming and going with cases of beer and heard the twang of country music coming through the door. Jimmie went in there, too. Nancy would hang around near the door, watching for him. When he'd come out, all chatty with a beer in his hand, he'd joke with her in his gravelly voice, spitting out his words rat tat tat tat tat tat, like out of a machine gun: "What are ya doin' with our dumb old Georgie? Sure, a girl like you needs a b'yfriend to take 'er out and show 'er a good time!"

Georgina knew her brother's game. "I'm telling ya, Nance. You'd better stop moonin' after Jimmy. He's a spiky townie. A little Graham's girl like you's gonna get some surprise if he decides to come on to ya."

"I'm not goin' to get no surprise. Don't forget, I've been out to the bunkers with Toughie. And, anyway, Jimmie told me he really likes me."

It was the Monday afternoon of Labour Day weekend, a moment caught in time between two seasons. The streets were bare of traffic, and the only movement was a few youngsters on front steps. Nancy's parents were both sleeping, her mother curled up tensely on the couch, her eyes shielded by the back of her hand; her father still holed up in the bedroom. In the bathroom, Nancy was busy applying makeup. She could hear her father turning over in bed, coughing and sighing.

Lately, the coughing had been getting worse. This morning when she brought in the tray, she'd noticed a spot of blood on the tissue he was grasping. Dad had opened his eyes and muttered to her in a strained voice, "Too bad you've got a sick old father, Nance."

"Don't worry, Dad, you're getting better," she'd said, in a hopeless attempt to soothe him.

Nancy opened the bathroom cabinet, took out her mother's perfume, "Sweet Surrender," and sprayed herself liberally.

She heard her father cough, then sigh again.

God, let me out of here.


For once, the Butler house was almost empty. Georgie wasn't even home. One of the little ones was playing ball on the veranda.

"Jimmie's inside watching TV," he said, as if he knew exactly what Nancy was after.

She went towards the front door, paused, then reached for the doorknob. It was loose and rattled as she pushed her way into the house. In the porch, she stopped again, fixed her skirt and patted her hair. Then she made a flash decision—flicking off her sandals, she put on a pair of Mrs. Butler's spikes. The hard arch of the high heels bit into her feet.

The living room was eerie, dead, like the eye of a storm. Jimmie was sitting on the sofa eating chips in a pool of ketchup, his fingertips red and gooey. Black and white cartoon characters chased around frantically on the TV screen but there was no sound.

"Hi, Nance. TV's on the blink again. Georgie's not here. Come on in anyway."

He was fully clothed but there was something fleshy, naked about him. The top buttons on his shirt were open, exposing a crucifix and a cluster of saints buried in his curly chest hair. The dark hair reminded Nancy of Tony Curtis, her favourite movie star. She edged her way into the chair by the door. He continued eating, muttering with his mouth full. "How's your father gettin' on? Don't see 'em around much."

He went into the kitchen, looking her directly in the eye as he passed. She sat there, not sure what to do. There was the sound of water running and the fridge door opening and closing. He was whistling "Teen Angel" and interrupted the tune to call out, "Why don't you come in here with me, girl."

An open beer stood on the table in front of him. He threw his head back and took a long swig of it, closing his eyes with pleasure as it went down his throat. Nance pinned herself against the counter, teetering on the red stilettos. He parted his lips in a half-smile as if he were about to tell a joke.

"Some fancy shoes you got on. What are you doin' dressed up like yer mother?"

He was lighting up a Lucky Strike.

"Wanna have a smoke while you're at it?"

He came over, took a nice long drag, blew a tantalizing billow her way, then slipped the cigarette between her lips. She took a few puffs, but couldn't stop sputtering and coughing. He took it out and threw it into the sink.

Now the decks were clear.

He put his hands on her breasts.

She caught her breath.

"Mmm…" he moaned, "I've been dyin' to get hold of these little tits."

Then he started nibbling her lips, softly. It was sweet. She closed her eyes, like in the movies. Before long, he was pressing harder, pushing her against the counter, barging in on her, his knee between her legs. She was scared, her heart pounding, but she liked the bristle of his beard, his warm breath, the feel of his grip.

"Come on in the backroom for a bit, will ya?" he said, his voice husky.


Once out of the kitchen, he got rougher, grabbing and poking as he kept up the necking. Her lips went numb until her only sensation was the taste of beer and tobacco in his mouth. They were crammed into an armchair. He was squashing her leg, but she didn't dare say anything. His rubbing and kissing was beginning to feel mechanical, impersonal, like he'd forgotten it was *her*—Nance, from two doors away.

She opened her eyes and, over his shoulder, had a look around the room. The curtains were closed and it was dim; all she could see were a few chairs, a radio, a single hospital style bed in the corner, and a band of bright daylight under the closed door. Jimmie tried to pull her towards the bed.

"I can't, Jimmie, I have to go home."

"I'm not gonna hurt ya."

But she froze in her cramped position on her side of the chair. He leapt up and leaned over her, parroting her, "Have to go home," his face contorted. "Go on then. You better go running back to your mother and that crazy bayman father you got."

Outside, there were footsteps in the hallway.

"Jimmie, are you in there drinking already?"

It was Georgina.

"Has Nance been over here? They're lookin' for her."

Nancy jumped up and fixed the straps on her top. The bedroom door flung open. Georgina stood in silhouette in the bright light of the hallway.

"That's not you in here with Jimmie! I told ya to stay clear of him. Your mudder'd be some mad if she knew the like of this was going on. Anyway, there's something wrong over to your place. You better go straight on home out of it."

"I didn't do nothin' to her," said Jimmie, hiding himself with his hands. Then he added in a cutting tone, "She's too stuck up for us."

Outside her house was an ambulance, its roof light spinning. They were just taking her father down the steps on a stretcher.

Her mother called out from the doorway. She looked neat in her starched apron but her colour was off.

"He took a bad turn, my child. But they're going to make him all better in the 'ospital. Come on in and 'ave your tea now. The minister's going to drop by for a word of prayer."

Nancy ran to the ambulance. As they lifted her father in, she thought she saw his hand motion to her. Her mind went straight to her favourite memory of him, at Nanny's funeral, when he'd held her little girl's hand in his big mechanic's hand. Already then, she knew how sorry he was about everything.

# CONSCIOUSNESS RAISING

YOUNG SHELEIGH, THE summer help in the office down to Ayre's, had taken to giving me advice. A year of "Women's Studies" at the university and she figured she knew it all, I guess. That was the new thing then, "women's liberation," and I was curious about it. So I let her preach away.

"You need to get out more, Georgina," she pronounced over lunch one Friday when I'd had a hell of a week. "Let your husband look after the kids. It's *your* life, Georgina. Women have to get hold of power."

I knew there was truth to what she was saying but I put her off.

"Power? I just want to get hold of some sleep!"

She unwrapped her health food sandwich—all sprouts and seeds. "Really, Georgina, my girlfriends and I are determined to take charge of our own lives."

I was intrigued by Sheleigh's hippie-commune life, another planet from mine, in council housing on Barter's Hill. Listening to her stories was pure entertainment for me. She shared a house with a bunch of hairy, half-washed students. They were crammed in there. Even the couch was rented out. And in the middle of all the ruckus and nightly partying, there were house rules about "equality."

"I know why you're so ground down, Georgina—you do all the housework and your husband goes scot-free. At our place, the boys have got to toe the line," she said, with a toss of her bossy little head. "Us girls are not picking up after them."

Lunch with Sheleigh in the windowless little staffroom had become a daily, eye-opening event for me. Some of her "women's lib" talk was shockin' beyond.

"Women wear themselves out trying to please *men*"—her voice got shrill when she said that word. "We should please ourselves. I don't have sex unless I really want it."

"Me neither," I mumbled, nearly choking on my egg sandwich.

My instinct with Sheleigh was motherly, but she kept putting me on her level, woman-to-woman, despite the fact that I was ten years older and had tons of raw experience with *men*. For sure I wasn't about to open up to her about what was going on in my marriage. I just kept skimming over the surface.

"Oh, Art thinks he's the king in the sex department, but I got news for him," I joked.

In those days, I was always joking around like that. Making out everything was okay with Art and me. But, in reality, we were just scraping by—on more levels than one. Art had a job in night security at the Lock-Up in the Courthouse but the salary was miserable. That's why I had to get out and work—on the phones, in the office down to Ayre's. What with the job, the two kids screaming when I got home, and Art out drinking (and probably carousing) whenever he got a chance, it was getting harder and harder to keep a brave face.

And who'd have thought that a young thing like Sheleigh would be the one to see through me?

Things were getting worse at home. Art was drinking more heavily. Then, one night when he was at work, my sister Janice came over to "talk" to me. It was ugly news: she knew for sure that Art had a girl on the go—a waitress from the Candlelight restaurant, a little duckie, as they say, barely out of school. I knew

Art had his dalliances, but I took the news hard—it wasn't that I was jealous of some little thing who'd be foolish enough to go out with Art, but just that it was one more piece of injustice in the hell that was my marriage. The next day, I went to work with makeup caked over the dark circles under my eyes.

Sheleigh leaned across the lunch table. "The makeup's not doing the job, Georgina. You look terrible. Is something wrong?"

"Oh, I was up with my little one all night," I answered as lightly as I could. "He's got that cold that's going around."

She gave me her woman-to-woman look. "Come on now, Georgina. Tell me what's goin' on."

I burst into tears. Told her she didn't know how lucky she was. Fussing over every little dropped stitch in her life. All that fancy talk she got on with. What a luxury!

Once I got going, I opened up full throttle.

"I've had a hard life, you know. Me and my sisters and brothers were dragged up by our mother. I thought when I got married I'd leave that all behind and make a nice home. I've been doing me best to be a good housekeeper. But it turns out I'm just stuck in prison with my kids and husband. Last night I found out that Art's cheating on me. And this is not the first time."

Sheleigh look shocked. For her, this was completely outrageous: A wife should simply not put up with such a thing from her husband.

I tried to explain, smooth things over: "Art's flirtations don't really matter to me. See, you don't stay 'in love' after you get married—there's kids to raise and other stuff to get on with. We'll be fine, we're just going through tough times." And I finished off with a lie. "I'm sure Art will see sense and stop his wandering."

That was a big slice of reality I was giving her. She was dumbfounded for a minute. But she rallied. "Listen, Georgina. I think you should join my CR group. It's a bunch of women who have frank discussions and help each other out."

I laughed as I wiped my tears. "What the hell is CR?"

"Consciousness raising. You share your feelings about your life, face up to how oppressed you are. It's liberating."

"Oh yeah, that's just what I need. Sharing my secrets with a bunch of girls I don't even know—what is it you call yourselves… feminists?" I pulled myself together.

"Never mind, my dear. I'm just havin' a bad day. And don't you breathe a word to anyone about what I told you. Art and I will work it out."

"Okay, okay," she said, sloughing me off. I could see she wanted to get back to that CR business. "Come on, now, Georgie. You've got to join the group. Learn about sisterhood and standing up for yourself. Why don't you come to this week's Friday meeting?"

It was good timing. Art had bullied his way into going off fishing that weekend. And I was ripe for something. The new little girlfriend was kind of a last straw.

On Friday at suppertime, Sheleigh turned up at our place, with a friend to babysit my youngsters. "Now get your duds on and let's go to the CR."

I took my apron off and changed, half excited and half scared to death.

Art would kill me if he knew what I was up to, I thought.

Then off I trotted behind Sheleigh. She had quite the stride in her ugly walking shoes. I had trouble keeping up—dressed as I was in my high heels that I wore on the few occasions I managed to get "out" anywhere.

"High heels are another whole issue," she threw back at me over her shoulder. "But that's for later."


The meeting was held in the living room of a little rented bungalow on Mayor Avenue. A student kind of a place, with sheets for curtains, almost no furniture, dirty cushions scattered around the floor, and the sickly sweet smell of incense in the air.

So this is how that crowd lives, I thought.

The other women were already sitting in a circle, some on the cushions and some on the few chairs. They were chatting and laughing, sharing their stories. I heard a snippet of one as I entered.

"He already had an erection but I…"

I froze in my tracks.

"Come on in and meet the others," said a kind of plumpish den mother with long hair down to her waist. She was wearing a "granny" dress and looked for the world like that rock star on TV—the one they call Mama Cass, who screams and writhes around when she sings.

I was surprised to see that the women weren't all young university types like Sheleigh. Two of them were older than me—one was kind of puckered looking, in a navy blue suit, like she'd just come from her job at the bank.

"This is my Aunt Marilyn," said Sheleigh. "It's her first night here, too."

What's she doing here? I thought.

"How do you do," she said formally.

"I'm grand, I s'pose," I replied, aware of the fact that I sounded like I was from Rabbittown.

Penny, the other older woman in the room, was wrinkly and grey-haired but decked out in those hippie clothes from the new little shops on Duckworth Street—embroidered shirt, long earrings, long skirt.

Mutton dressed as lamb, I thought. What the *hell* is she doing here?

The rest of the group were cut from the same cloth as Sheleigh. Intense little faces, lithe bodies, small breasts free of bras, nipples showing through T-shirts.

The Mama Cass look-alike, who'd apparently shed her real name and was now known as *Jade*, lit a stick of incense, then sat on a cushion and crossed her legs.

"Thanks for coming, everybody," she said in a sugary voice. "Let's begin by holding hands and saying a sisterhood poem."

Hold hands with a woman? I was mortified. And, to boot, I was perched on one of the chairs alongside crusty old Aunt Marilyn. Her hand was bony and cold and all the way through the prayer (*surviving the hurricanes of life, in sisterhood we…*) I was worried she'd notice my rough palms—housemaid's skin from washing diapers.

"Now then," said Mama Jade, swaying her long hair. "We have a list of questions. Each one of us gets to answer, then we have general discussion." She opened a copy of *Ms. Magazine* to a marked page and read: "How do you deal with sharing household chores with your male partner?"

Aunt Marilyn the banker jumped in. "Jeffry never came into the kitchen or cleaned the house. That was my domain. Now I suppose, since he's living with that young thing, he's probably changed his ways and helping out." She looked like she was sucking a lemon. "I know for damn sure, I'm glad I've just got myself to clean up after. Like they say, *It'll have to be some man to be better than no man.*"

"I think it's time we stopped making the kitchen a female fortress," said Alison, with the halo of curly blond hair. I recognized her from the news on TV. She led the protests against women being "sexually harassed" by their bosses. Brave girl, I'd thought. I should be marching with her. My boss in the office touched me sometimes, little flicks on my back around to the side of my tits. But I never did anything about it. What was the use? That stuff is as old as the hills. Who's ever going to stop it?

Next up was the over-aged hippy, Penny. Now this one had it all sorted out. Her husband was a retired accountant and stayed home doing housework while she went out golfing in the summer and curling in the winter. No doubt, she was the toast of the town.

"Fred peels the potatoes and shines the brass," she said, her earrings dangling. "Then he goes over the whole place with the carpet sweeper. By the time I get home for supper everything is spic and span. I discovered women's lib a long time ago. That's why I came to this group, to see if you girls had anything new to offer. So far, I think I could teach you a lesson or two."

Well, la de da, I thought.

Another skinny little one called Polly piped up with a long diatribe—like a set piece you'd recite in a school play. She and her live-in, "Carlo," (she'd somehow found an Italian in St. John's) had drawn up a plan to share housework. Complete equality. They had a monthly roster posted with a magnet on the fridge.

"And this Carlo pulls his weight?" asked the bitter Aunt Marilyn. "Actually does the chores?"

Polly went all noble and temple-like. "Well, I have to be very patient. Carlo was spoiled by his Italian mother. Never had to lift a finger. He's a hopeless cook and he's after burning the bottom out of most of our pots. And today he was supposed to sweep up, but when I came home he explained he couldn't find the broom. I didn't get mad at him—we looked for the broom together."

I couldn't believe what I was hearing. She didn't know where the broom was?

Sheleigh nodded in my direction. My turn had come.

"Art's got one of them mothers, too. Tended on him hand and foot. I shudders when I thinks of her. Mrs. Perfect Housekeeper. When we got married she gave me the recipes for Art's favourite dishes. But when I try to make them dishes, Art complains they're not as good as his mother's. Art don't do nothing around the house. To be honest with you, I can't be bothered getting him to help. Like they says, you might as well get the cat to do it. He only does it wrong and I have to take over. What's the use?"

Sheleigh got preachy about how unfair my life was, working all day, looking after the kids and, on top of that, doing all the housework. "Why don't you get Art to do one chore and report back to us next time how it went? You have to begin somewhere."

I didn't answer, just got a knot in my stomach at the thought of it.

Ethel, a tall lanky girl with shiny black eyes—Sheleigh had told me she was an ex-nun—made a confession that she was letting herself be a doormat with her fella, a "medieval scholar," she called him.

"Jonathan's got his head in the stratosphere all the time. It's hard to nudge him towards the dishes."

She looked tense, poor thing. How could she take a few dishes so seriously?

She finished off with a sigh. "I should confront him about the dishes. I feel guilty for being so weak."

"Women and guilt is a whole other question," said Mama Jade, hauling herself up from her cushion. "I think it's time for a little drink."

Then we stopped the discussion and they broke open the bottles of wine. We all stood in the kitchen. It was pretty sticky in there. Even I could see that the counters were bawling out for a good swipe.

The girls were all friendly but I felt uncomfortable about being the only one who didn't seem to be on the right page about housework, and I even had CR homework to do. So I had too much to drink and got overly talkative and ended up telling stories about Art.

"On payday, when he gets drunk, I take his keys and lock him in the house while I bring the kids over to his mother's. Me and the kids go down the street and he calls out the window after me, like a youngster, 'Georgie, let me out!' And the neighbours can hear him. 'Got him barred in again,' they say, 'Proper thing.'"

The girls were having a grand time because I can spin a yarn and wine makes me funny as hell, if I do say so myself. And, let's face it, that crowd needed a little loosening up.

"Art would kill me if he heard me talking like this," I kept saying. "He'd kill me!"

And they'd all go off into gales of laugher.

I guess I was enjoying the shock value and the attention they were giving me. But all the while I was joking, it was hurting me like knife pain. Art and his drinking and all the work I had to do to keep me and the kids going was pressing me down real bad. But I kept on making a joke of it.

"Art wouldn't know a broom from his arse—let alone a carpet sweeper—but he knows his way around the sheets, if you know what I mean."

The second that came out of my mouth, I hated myself for saying it.

"My Fred is a whiz with the carpet sweeper," said perfect Penny. She had a little buzz on, the wine had warmed her up. "But he's useless in the sheets."

I was getting uncomfortable with the sheets thing. "Oh, don't get me wrong! Art's no Romeo," I said, with a forced laugh.

Penny caught my eye for a minute, as if she knew the ugliness behind my joking.

On the way home, everything I'd said about Art came rushing over me. Why did I have to open my big mouth like that?

"I can't come back to the CR, Sheleigh. They're nice enough but this is not my crowd. And how am I going to do that homework—get Art to help out?"

"Come on, Georgina, give it a go." She was playing the adult with me again. "You can do it!"

At the next meeting, I was first on the carpet. The girls were eager to know if I managed to get Art to pick up a dishtowel. I started out apologetic, running off at the mouth about how the playoffs were on and I couldn't pry Art away from the TV, let alone get him to do housework, and how Art's mother was coming for supper last night and there I was again, slavin' away, youngsters crawling around my legs, rushing to get the food together to please her.

Mama Jade picked up the *Ms. Magazine* and showed the group an article about competitive mothers-in-law who know nothing about sisterhood and sharing.

"Competitive," I said, laughing. "Art's mother'd rather skin ya than share—especially her precious son.

"Anyway, last night, the homework for you girls was on my mind as I took the lemon fluff pudding out of the oven. Art was at the table having a beer. His team had won and he was in a good mood, in the happy drunk phase. So I sweet talked him. 'Listen darlin', I still got to do the salads and set the table. Why don't you whip that cream for me?' He balked at first but then got up and put my apron on, turning it all into a big spoof, making outrageous poufy poses. I set him up with the beaters and a chilled bowl and he started in.

"'Is that enough?' he kept shouting over the whirl of the beaters.

"'Keep going until it's stiff,' I called from the other room.

"'That sounds good,' he joked.

"A few minutes later he came over and showed me the bowl—he'd beaten the cream into butter. 'Never mind,' I said. 'I got more cream in the fridge. I'll whip it.' And I did."

"That was a mistake, Georgina. You should have made him do it," said Sheleigh, quoting from her book of rules, "Men make a mess of things so you won't ask for help again. I've seen that trick."

"You missed an opportunity to stand your ground," added Polly, ever so righteous.

I didn't know what to say. Just shrugged my shoulders. I felt like a youngster in school—the nuns rapping me on the knuckles for getting me sums wrong.

Mama Jade picked up her list of questions.

Thank God I'm off the hot seat, I thought.

"Are you free to express yourself sexually or does your partner dominate?" she said, point blank.

I let out a spontaneous hoot. Then put my hand over my mouth. I'd vowed to keep a lid on it at tonight's meeting.

Polly went first. She and Carlo had perfect equality in bed. He was all into women's sexual expression, vaginal orgasm, clitorises, etc.

I blushed, felt the heat rise in my cheeks.

Blessed Virgin, what am I going to say when my turn comes? I can't go talking about clitorises and Art...

Ethel, the ex-nun, looking mousy and pained, admitted that she was "still mixed up about sex." Jonathan has to help her along—and he's "not all that sexy, really."

Sheleigh got right to the point, as usual. She used to "fake orgasms" to please her boyfriend. But not anymore. And she felt *so* much better about herself.

"Jeffry was in and out quick," said Aunt Marilyn. "I hardly had time to get going. I s'pose that new young thing makes him linger. The thought of it makes me sick, to be honest with you."

Too UNSPEAKABLE for Words

My turn came. Here I was with my load of truth again. I was nervous, my throat was tight and I had to keep clearing it. But I said my piece.

"Fake orgasm? That's the least of my worries. I'm just desperate to keep Art away from me. The last thing I need is another youngster coming along. We're Catholic, see, and not allowed to use the Pill. He comes home from night shift at six in the morning and crawls into bed, waking me up from my precious sleep, tormenting me for 'a little nooky' before he drops off. 'Give it up Art,' I says, 'I don't want to get pregnant again.' But he keeps at me till he gets his way."

"You can't go on like this," said Penny, like she was in charge of me.

Then all hell broke loose with the advice. How there's a clinic where they give out the Pill, no questions asked. How even Catholic women can get it.

"I'd be afraid to be seen goin' into one of those places," I said.

"I volunteer there," said Ethel. "Lots of Catholic women come in."

"Well, I'm not *lots of Catholic women*."

"I'll go with you," said earnest young Alison.

"Yeah, Georgina," chimed in Mama Jade, "go with her. You don't have to have more kids if you don't want to."

They were ganging up on me. The story of my life—people shovin' me around. I'd had enough.

"I'm not going to no clinic," I said, plain as I could.

Still determined to take me over, Penny said she'd make an appointment for me with a Protestant doctor who'd put me on the Pill, *no questions asked*.

I was terrified of the blasphemy, as if the priest was in the room, listening.

"Protestant doctor! I can't be doin' that. I've seen Dr. Dougherty all my life."

I was getting shaky.

Penny came over and sat by me. She put her arm around my shoulder. I wriggled on the hard chair while she went on and on about Catholic doctors just wanting women to keep popping out youngsters. And how the times were changing and I had to get with it.

The younger ones were all waving their heads in agreement.

They're all on the Pill, I thought. Little over-sexed duckies, probably at it every night.

Then Sheleigh did the hell and all.

"I know you asked me not to mention this, Georgie, but don't you think it's time to liberate yourself and face up to the truth about Art, especially his cheating? Why don't you let the others know how bad it is. You shouldn't have to put up with that. It's disgusting how your husband…"

I jumped up.

"Is that what you call *sisterhood*, tellin' stories out of school? And what the hell do you know about youngsters and husbands and being Catholic?"

I shouted at the top of my lungs, "None of ye know nothing!"

I went to the door. Penny came right after me, patting my arm and telling me I was right to be upset, that they'd been too hard on me and she'd give me a ride home.

In the car, I was puffing and blowing and fiddling with my purse.

We reached my house.

"Thanks for the ride. I never should have gone there."

Penny put her hand on my twitchy fingers.

"Yes, you should have. Every woman has a right to share her story."

My stomach was heaving.

I can't stand any more of this CR talk, I thought.


I got home to an empty house. The kids were at my mother-in-law's for the weekend and Art was God knows where. Probably with that girl. I sat at the kitchen table. What a state I was in. Crying down tears like a baby. Retching from the gut.

Sheleigh's right. Why am I hiding the truth about Art?

I went back to the argument we'd had earlier. "Where do you think you're going?" he'd said. "Pawning the kids off on Mom again. I heard you say something about a 'women's group' to your sister. Is that what you're up to? What do that bunch of bitches be talking about?"

I pictured him, batting his eyelashes like he does when he's nervous. He's not all that stupid, I thought. He knows something's brewing with me.

The phone rang. It was Penny, checking to see if I was okay.

I cried into the phone. "It's true, he runs around with other women. The only way out is to leave him. I knows that."

"Listen, Georgina. I left my first husband. It's not easy to untangle a marriage. I'm here if you need me."

"That's all right," I blurted, afraid of her Protestant remedies. "I can manage."

I hung up.

Art came home, in his cups, feeling amorous. "Let's go to bed," he said, grabbing hold of me.

I pushed him away. He came in on me, opening the buttons on my blouse. "What's wrong with you. Come on to bed, we got no kids to bother us."

I got away from him. Then I steeled myself, stood on my two feet and said it.

"Art, I'm leaving you." I can still hear how my voice wobbled.

He looked at me in utter surprise. "Ah! Come on, Georgie. Don't go getting like that."

I did up the buttons on my blouse. "I can't stand it anymore. I'm finished with ya, Art. I knows about all those young girls you chase after."

At first, he pleaded and begged. "I don't mean to be cheating on ya, Georgie. It's just a bit of fun." Tears shot into his eyes. "I promise I'll be faithful from now on." The pleading went on for a while. "And I'm going to cut down on the drinking. I swear that's the end of it. I'm going be with you and you only. I'll never cheat on you again."

I let him finish, then stood my ground. "Yes, you will. You

can't help yourself. It's all over, Art. I'm getting out."

This time, he heard the finality in my voice. He was stunned for a second, but then the rage rose up in him. He banged the wall with his fist. "No you're not. You are not going anywhere. No way! Them bitches got ya all churned up."

His eyelashes were batting like crazy. "I'm barrin' ya in the house until you change your mind."

He locked the door, took my keys, and ripped the phone off the wall. After all the times I'd barred him in, he had me good and locked down.

Sit it out, I thought. He'll fall asleep and I'll escape.

He slept on the couch, snoring and snorting. I tried to get the key out of his pocket but he woke up. "You're not going nowhere. You're my *wife*, get it?"

The siege lasted until Sunday morning. Finally, while he was sleeping off the beer he'd drunk on Saturday night, I opened the bathroom window a crack and called out to one of the neighbours. "Call the police. Art got me locked in here against my will. He's drunk and I'm scared."

The police banged on the door. The loudest bang I've ever heard.

"OPEN UP! POLICE!"

Art woke up and shot me a look of pure hatred. It's funny, but, at that moment, I felt sorry for him.

In came the officers. Two of them, big and burly, in their RNC uniforms with all the paraphernalia hanging off them.

"What's goin' on Art, b'y?" said one of them clapping Art on the back. "Having trouble with the wife?"

I might have known. Working down at the Lock-Up, Art knew all the officers.

The policeman looked at me. "Are you sure you need us here, my love?"

I'd had all weekend to get my mind good and clear. "I want to press charges," I said, "for forced confinement, or whatever you call it."

A year later, legally separated, I made a return visit to the CR group. After all, they were the ones who got me going.

I sat on that same hard chair and told them my tale—the doubts, the costs, the hurt. No more hiding the truth behind my pathetic jokes.

"It's been a rough year but Art and I are out of our misery."

The girls were glowing with amazement. My little hard-liner friend, Sheleigh, who I hadn't seen since she finished her job at Ayre's in the fall, stood up and paid tribute to me. "We were wrong to gang up on you. You're not supposed to do that in a CR group. But look at you now. You're the one who really turned herself around."

"We're still working away at our issues," said Mama Jade, picking up her *Ms. Magazine*.

Oh, no! I thought, they're going to start in with those questions.

Mama Jade read from her list: "Can men be feminists or do they always ultimately play the man's game?"

"I wouldn't trust a man who says he's a feminist," said Aunt Marilyn, still sucking the lemon. "They just can't help being what they are."

"My Fred's a feminist," said Penny, as self-satisfied as ever. "He'd never try to override me."

God help poor long-suffering Fred! I thought.

"I have my ups and downs with Carlo," said the ever-patient Polly, "He does his best but he *is* Italian. He can be really macho. I'm trying to get him to join a men's CR but he won't hear of it."

I let out one of my hoots. "Men's CR. I'd like to be a fly on the wall for that one. What do they talk about? Car engines?"

The joke fell into dead air. I glanced around the circle. They all had that intense look, revving up for discussion.

"Well, good luck to you trying to make men into feminists! It's hard enough being one yourself!" I stood up.

"Now come on, girls. I came here to celebrate. Let's go into the kitchen and open the wine. And I'll tell you about my new man. Carpet sweeper and all."

# NO TEARS

I GREW UP on Cape Verde Island, in the heyday of the cod fishery, as a daughter of a prosperous fish merchant. That was a big deal in those days. My father was revered by almost everyone on the island. And at home, he demanded adulation. Whatever he said, went.

We're all sitting around the fire in the front room. Dark winter's afternoon. Snap of cold outside. Sound of footsteps crunching in the snow on the front porch. Mother stiffens.

"That's your father coming in now."

As he opens the door, there's a draft of cold air and a great clatter. Youngsters running to fetch things. His voice booming.

"Hurry up, now. I want to settle in and hear the news on the wire."

I still think back on those moments. They had a certain order to them. You knew how things would go.

Mother had five of us and then spent the rest of her life "feeling poorly." As the eldest child, and not in any way a frivolous girl, I stepped in as lady-of-the-house. I was barely eighteen, but Father had no hesitation when it came to my capabilities.

"You'll have to oversee the little ones now," he muttered, not even looking up from his newspaper. "Your mother's got to get her rest."

She's in her room with the curtains drawn, sitting up in bed. I go in and tidy up, then bring the younger children in to see her briefly. Each child leans in to kiss her cool cheek; she asks them a few vague questions, then I shepherd them out of the dimmed room. Outside, they squint in the brightness of the hallway and that's the end of the visit for the day.

It wasn't long before I'd turned the house into my own fiefdom. The place was shipshape. I lit a fire under the help, Bernice, a surly-faced girl but an excellent cook. A full dinner was served promptly at noon every day, and peppermint knobs sat permanently in a dish on the dining room sideboard.

And then, of course, there were my younger siblings to keep in line. Facing their resentment, I became the complete agent of my father's authority, corralling and correcting them. A thankless task. But I ran the place with an iron rule.

"Come on, now, Maura. Father says you're wasting too much time with that singing." My sister's got the musicality from mother's side of the family. "It's time you got away from that piano. Go do your homework."

"You're just jealous. I'm going to marry an artist and go to New York to train my voice."

"That'll be the day. Who's ever going to listen to the like of you?"

"God, you're cold. Frozen like a glacier. No man's ever gonna go near you. You'll end up a bitter old maid."

*Old maid*—the unkindest cut of all. I could feel the sting of it. Like all young girls, I was under pressure to attract a man and get married. It followed me around like a fuzzy shadow. There was no sloughing it off. I blame the women. They're the ones who keep it all going, with their wedding fever. They're bound to keep asking and prying.

"Do you have a young man yet, my dear?"

My cousin Priscilla's engagement party. Little sandwiches with the crusts cut off. Tea in china cups. Aunt Ginny in her glory. She's trilling.

"Come see the dress—we had it sent down from Montreal. It's French lace."

I go into the room with the other girls; they're all tittering and frothy. I'm a dead weight. They seem so foolish. Of course, most girls have a wedding dress floating around in their imagination. Just ask them and they'll tell you exactly what they're going to wear down the aisle. And I have to admit, a flicker of a dress did come into my mind that day—a satin gown, clean lines, no fuss. But I had a way of not letting those thoughts take over. People spill their emotions at every tick of the clock. Upset about this, longing for that. But not me—I've always kept a lid on it, best I could. I knew what they all said, that I was "gawky" and "frigid" with "no marriage prospects." So be it. I had a household to run.

Maura's never forgiven me for not taking her side with the singing. But I had to agree with Father. To this day, she's a foolish girl with a head full of pipe dreams and given to melodrama. Mind you, back in those days, Father himself could be the biggest culprit of all for bringing upset into the house. And then, despite the so-called grip I had on myself, I too would succumb to the drama, my feelings curled up like tight little springs inside me.

I'm in the back pantry, in a cold sweat, with bad cramps, but no tears. All my life, I've been plagued with those cramps.

Tonight, Father's in one of his rages. Revered in the Bay he may be, but there are those who despise him, and when his authority is questioned, a monster rises up. He has that vicious face on him, ghostly white with arched eyebrows. And he's roaring like a bull: "No goddam fishermen's union's going to tell me how to do business."

Now the children are awake. I can hear them scrambling across the floorboards upstairs. They call down to me.

"Go to sleep," I call back, "nothing to worry about."

I go into the kitchen, need to busy myself. Father calls out from the front room, "Someone there?"

His voice has gone thin. Sounds like the anger is spent, thank God.

"It's okay, Father, just the wind at the back door."

Slowly, I recover from the sweats, shove those dark feelings aside, get back to the task at hand. Try to make it all jell, like a tricky blancmange for a Sunday night.

And that's how I live. Keeping a lid on it.


It's the annual parish garden party. I go along but more as a mother than as a bride-for-the-offering. Other girls are sitting at the booths, selling raffle tickets, flirting with the boys. But I'm in the back of the dinner tent, arranging the sit down teas, supervising the slicing of the turkey and the divvying up of the salads. And this I do to perfection. In charge. Truly my "father's daughter" as they all keep saying. I guess nothing's changed in that department.

I still go back to that moment in the tent, the smell of trodden-down grass, yeasty homemade bread and tea bags. It's a sunny day but wild, the wind billowing in the sides of the canvas, the occasional gust lifting the tablecloths, displaying the trestles underneath.

As busy as I am with the teas, from time to time I cast an eye in the direction of the high jinks going on around the Wheel of Fortune. The big attraction this year is a group of soldiers from the American base. Big Yanks, with their toothy smiles and crew cuts, head and shoulders over the rest of the crowd.

Something is pulling me to look over there at those men.

Just as I am about to call ticket holders to take their seats, there's one unholy gust from the northwest and the whole works blows over, tent and all. Shattered dishes, Jello and Spanish Cream all over the place. I step to the fore and take over, directing the other young people and soldiers, who pitch in to clean up.


When the tent is up again, the trestles restored and tea brewed, I sit down.

"Can I offer you a cup of tea?" A twangy American accent. He's blond and big-framed, but not handsome: little gray eyes magnified by thick, steel-rimmed glasses. I take the tea. He slides in next to me on the bench. I can sense his leg next to mine.

"Okay if I join you, Miss? John Slater from Chichi, Texas, flat and dusty, home of Wilden tractors."

He's soft-spoken and his warmth flows all over me. Already I'm in a little cocoon with him. I'm not used to such proximity— we don't touch in the McGrath family. He stretches his arm along the back of the bench, almost embracing me.

"Beautiful event you put on here. You sure did a great job of making it all happen. Are you from the island?"

I tell him who I am. Speak of my father being a prominent merchant, our big family. He looks out over Cape Verde—the harbour full of boats, the hills and barrens in the distance—and admires the McGrath house, surrounded by its own rolling fields. His arm is touching the hair on the back of my head. I feel the glacier in me begin to melt, just a trickle. I shift to the edge of the bench, try to shut myself down. But I keep talking. On and on I go about the family: The McGraths are this, the McGraths are that.

"You know, you remind me of my mother," he says with a

sunny, smile. "So capable, always taking care of everybody. I really admire that."

No doubt I was carried away by male attention, flattered by the thought that maybe I wasn't such a gawky old maid after all. I did feel some sort of relief, to find myself acting, for once, like the other girls. But that was short-lived.

With the setting sun, the wind drops, the sky goes purple and the picnic grounds empty out. Most of the soldiers have linked up with girls. I'm still sitting there with the Texan. He's doing the talking now.

"My Mom's the brains of the family. She runs the whole ranch."

I'm interested, but still keeping my distance. That distance.

"Come on, you two," says Jennie Hiscock, who comes to our door selling eggs and normally would never speak to me like that. "We're all goin' out on the barrens for a bonfire."

I get up from the bench. I don't be going places with the likes of Jennie Hiscock. And I've heard of what goes on at those bonfires.

"Sounds like real fun," says John Slater, taking my hand as he stands up.

I slip my hand out of his. My heart pounds. "I have to get back to the house…"

"Oh! Please don't go home now, Miss Faith McGrath," he says, puffing God-knows-what my way. "You're such good company. And it's a beautiful night."

Defying my own good sense, with the glacier in me already rehardening, I went out there with that man.

Full moon on the barrens, blue light spilling over the rocks. The Texan and I lag behind the crowd as they head for the pond, singing. He puts his big thick arm around my waist.

"Come here," he says, pulling me in like he owns me. "Let yourself have a good time." I look out into the barrens, get a nervous cramp. How am I ever going to get home out of this?

Tongues of smoke swirl into the air as they light the bonfire. Boughs crackle and the fire roars. I can see the murmuring silhouettes of the other couples, settling into serious courting. They're smooching and squirming and the soldiers are touching the girls all over.

He takes me into a bear hug. Starts kissing me. A strange mushy sensation. I can taste his chewing gum. So this is what kissing feels like. He's intent on the necking. I try to give something back, but I can't.

Jennie Hiscock calls across the fire, "I knows the young missus likes American kisses." Then, "Make sure you invite me to the weddin' now. I got to see that one."

I un-stick my lips from his. "I'm going back, right now."

"Ah, don't mind the others," he says in that softie way of his that's beginning to grate. "They're not worth half of you. Let's get away from them."

"I need to go home."

"Come on over here with me and we'll start going."

I go along with him.

We wander to the edge of a starlit pond. He sits on a big boulder, pulls me down next to him. In the reeds, a bird stirs, starts peeping.

"The stars are almost in our lap," he says, all romantic. Then he comes in close, kisses me again. I sputter, try to push him away. He grabs hold of my arms, his thumbs pressing like two nails going into me.

"Nothing to be afraid of, you know. You're a grown-up girl, a real woman. What do you think we came out here for?"

He pushes me down and before I know it, he's on top of me, pushing my skirt up, pulling my panties down. I remember the weight of him on me and the rough scratch of the rock underneath. And then, the filling-a-hole sensation of his member inside me, a moan, a big poke and then out. And that was it.

I shimmy myself back into my panties and sit up. Flecks of blood on the hem of my dress and a deep red streak of morning on the horizon.

The others are moving off, laughing across the emptiness.

"I'm going straight home," I say, embarrassed by the frog in my throat, the whole mortifying event.

He looks up at the sky. "What's the rush? Let's stay and watch the sun come up!"

I set out, trudging along through the berry bushes in my party shoes. He walks alongside me, trying to chat. But I walk ahead and refuse to look at him.


Dawn and I'm back in my father's house. The garden party dress is burning in the coal stove. I'm standing in the kitchen in my slip, when the maid, Bernice, turns up for work. She looks me up and down with wide eyes. "Are you all right?" she says, definitely more curious than concerned. The last thing I need is her sticking her nose in. She's been party to too many family secrets as it is.

"I just came down to light the stove to make tea," I say, heading for the door before she notices the two thumb-mark bruises on my arms.


Father made one and only one remark when the baby started to show.

"You'll not go out during the confinement. The orphanage will take it at birth."

I knew that Father would permit no expression of sentiment about the child. His own father before him was much the same—stiff old Grandpa McGrath, snapped shut to anything that might disturb the order of things, bring shame or messy emotion. So we carried on with our lives. Ignoring my big bump. Even my littlest siblings knew implicitly never to refer in any way to the state I was in. Only in the privacy of my room would I place my hands around my belly and feel the baby kicking. In those stolen moments, I did let myself enjoy the new life in my body, my cheeks flushed and breasts swelling.

On a mild spring night with the bedroom window open, I gave birth, upstairs in my father's house. It happened fast, a few hard pangs and the baby slipped out. As I lay on the bed, in all the goo and birth mess, the doctor took the child from me and passed it to my father. He went straight down the stairs and out the door to a car that was waiting with the engine running. I heard him say "girl" to someone out there in the dark, then he came back in, closed the door and turned the lock.

For a while after, I felt hollow, barren, except of course, for my leaking breasts. Who would have thought that someone as dry as myself could produce so much milk? But that all passed. Then came the longings, wanting to see the child, painful urges I could barely tolerate. But with time, I found a way to contain all that in an enduring fantasy—she and I in a lush garden, the kind you see on placemats and calendars. Again and again, I let myself float off into that one scene, so far from any reality I would ever know: the two of us together, myself with a little girl in a white summer dress.


Then I moved on to another fantasy.

It's the Christmas concert at the Basilica in St. John's—the Mercy Convent Girls' Choir. For the third carol, a soloist steps forward, a skinny little girl in a stiff convent uniform. I immediately sense something familiar about her: Is it her dark hair? Her eyes? Her long arms? I glance at the concert programme and find her name—*Edith Quinn, Grade V*. I stretch my neck and peer over the heads in the front rows to get a clearer view. With a cramp in my belly, I listen hard to the child's rendition of "Silent Night." Even the timbre of her voice, the way she draws her breath, sounds intimate, familiar. She's got presence, this little girl performing in perfect pitch under the huge vaulted ceiling.

For years after, I heard her singing in my mind. And I kept picturing her face, her lips enunciating the words… *Round yon virgin mother and child.*

After mother and father died and the fishery on Cape Verde went down, I sold the McGrath house. It was a grand old place and my siblings wanted to keep it, for the glory of the McGraths. But that wasn't practical. No sense hanging on to the past. It's been turned into a B & B now, and that's well and good.

Once the estate was settled, I moved to town and took this position as Superintendent at the Nurse's Residence. Perfect job. Lots to oversee.

In the evenings, I retire upstairs to my old-maid's quarters, with no one to bother me. Except that image on TV. Edith Quinn. There she is. All grown up. And quite an accomplished singer. Always on the screen for the special shows at Christmas and Paddy's Day, singing away with her hands clasped, playing to the camera on the high notes.

I know for sure it's her. Those are my eyes, dark and velvety like some Arabian princess. It runs in the family—God knows where that ever came from. She's got my physique too. Prominent collarbones you can see along the neckline of her dress. And, of course, she's got the musicality from mother's side of the family. What a voice. She can really belt it out. They say she's been invited to try out for the chorus at the Met.

Edith Quinn. I can watch her forever, admire her at a nice comfortable distance. My own child, a fine young woman in all her fullness, not just a thin voice in my head. It all turned out good in the end. No mess, no fuss.

It's a slushy old February night with the wind beating the shutters. I'm just boiling the kettle for me and my sister Maura. She's in town from Burin to see the specialist. I'll be glad when she's gone. Too much chat and still going on about becoming a singer. I'm weary tonight. There's been trouble all day in the residence. One of the nurses has been kicked out for having a man in her room. Her friends are bawling to have the decision reversed. I've had enough of this nonsense.

A light knock on the door. A pause. Then another, louder, knock. I open it a crack. It's a youngish woman, in a fancy camel-hair coat—not bought here in town, for sure. She's blond with gray eyes and she's tall, broad shouldered, like a man.

"Yes," I bark.

"Sorry to knock unannounced but are you Miss Faith Mc-Grath?" The voice is exaggeratedly soft, incongruous with her manly build.

"What's this now?"

"So sorry. My name is Laura Lewis. I need to talk to you about something personal."

A shadow flits across my mind. Makes me open the door. As she enters, she says "Sorry" a couple of more times in a breathy voice. Now she's sitting in my armchair. I'm not used to that—a complete stranger in my private nest. I don't invite her to take her coat off.

"Now then." I can hear my own sharpness. "What's this all about?"

Maura's settled onto the couch, all ears and curiosity. Big silly smile on her face.

Out comes the story. Whoever she is, she's a talker. Out of control. And soppy: "I moved to the mainland years ago... married a doctor in Moncton...but I've been longing all my life...have never felt like I belong...can't see myself in anybody... wonder who I am...now my two children want to know their background...."

My chest is getting tight, little needles pricking me. And to think I was convinced that Edith Quinn was the one. Had her all tucked away in a neat place in my mind. Now this.

But there's no denying it. Laura Lewis is the spit of him: the blond hair, and of course, the big Texas bones. And she's got that same warmth spilling out of her. Reminds me how I got roped into making the mistake of my life, all those years ago.

She pulls the birth documents out of her purse and passes them to me. I glance at them, see my name, typewritten, with a flying F on Faith. I put them on my lap. They drop onto the floor.

Of course, Maura was right there to pick them up. She reads them.

"Oh my goodness, you really are a long lost McGrath." Then looking askance at me, "Don't you worry, my dear, you've found us now. We'll welcome you into the family."

Maura's getting her own back, I think, making offers I'll never live up to.

Laura Lewis keeps looking at me. Doe-eyed. Expectant. She can look as hard as she wants; she'll never find her blond self in me.

"That was all a long time ago," I say, with not a hint of emotion. God knows I'm skilled at nipping a topic I don't want to hear of. I can see she feels the chill I'm giving off. For a split second I hesitate, almost try to warm up a degree, but I draw back. It's too late for that now. After all this time, I'm locked inside myself. Can't get out.

"You've had your life and I've had mine," I add, in a final attempt to push her away. "Especially with you living on the mainland for so many years."

She looks like she's about to start whimpering. I make a small false effort.

"Lewis. Is that your maiden name? Do you get home much? It must be nice living in New Brunswick."

That's the best I can do. I can't, won't, ever go back to the night on the barrens. There's a speck of anger in her now. Her voice is trembling.

"I know this is a shock but can you at least tell me who my father is?"

Maura stirs in her chair. Old codes are being broken here. Not even my siblings know for sure who did that to me. I take a deep breath.

"He was an American soldier from Texas. Name of John Slater. You've got his likeness from what I remember. It was an accident. He doesn't know you exist, that's for sure. You can look for him in a town called Chichi."

Maura passes the documents back to her. The thick papers crinkle as she stuffs them into her purse. I stand up with finality.

"You must come see us in Burin," says Maura, still digging at me.

Laura Lewis makes her way to the door. "Well, goodbye," she croaks, tears streaming.

Maura puts her hand on Laura's shoulder. "Don't forget, you're welcome anytime."

I stay back.

"So long, now," I manage.

It's just as well she lives away.

# FAIRY-LED

BERNICE CAN'T STOP wringing her hands. "I was just tryin' to give the poor little one some company."

The pastor puts his hand on her shoulder. "You mustn't fret about the accident. You're not to be blamed for what happened."

She crosses her thick legs, tries to look feminine, needy. "Those McGraths are blaming me for everything. Even for telling a few old stories. I spent my life serving that family, and they've up and fired me. Oh my! I can't help frettin'."

"There's no need, my dear." He sits down next to her, unbuttoning the jacket of his oversized suit. "God loves you. You're not alone."

She stays in the same vein. Her voice wobbles. "It's lonely up in that cottage away from everybody. They says you can be fairy-led, coaxed away up there. But I knows that's old nonsense. There's no such thing as fairies. It's just the dead quiet nights with the light leaving the hills."

It was a June morning that Meredith, the youngest of the McGrath girls, who was married to a St. John's merchant, had turned up at the house in Cape Verde with Sharon by the hand.

Bernice was cleaning the front windows and watched the two of them come up the walkway. The little six-year-old was dawdling and Meredith was yanking her arm.

Meredith's rough on that child, thought Bernice. Not much of a mother.

Faith, the old-maid sister who ran the McGrath household, opened the door to them.

"Oh! Dear God! Faith!" wailed Meredith, holding her hand to her throat, like she barely had the strength to talk. "I just came straight out here on the early ferry. We've got a situation on our hands."

Faith rushed them into the living room.

Bernice positioned herself to get the details through the closed door. Over the years, she'd listened in on many a heated debate between the McGraths.

"Try to calm down and see sense, Meredith," said Faith, ever the older sister. "I know you have your worries, with a husband like Mike…but honestly, parking that child out here for the length of the holidays…"

"You've got to take her, Faith. The doctor put me on the nerve pills."

"But there's no youngsters fit for her to play with on the Cape—they're all a crowd of ruffians out here. A shy redhead like Sharon will die of loneliness stuck in this house. And, of course, I'm the one who'll be saddled with the supervising."

Poor youngster, thought Bernice, being supervised by that witch, Faith. The child will die of loneliness for sure.

Meredith lowered her voice. "I'm telling you right now, I simply can't have her. You don't know the worst of it. It's not just that Mike went with that young maid Jessie. He up and got her pregnant! We had to send her home to her people. Imagine, a serving girl having a child of Mike's. He's gone out of the house now. And I'm not fit to look after a youngster. I can't have her."

"A shocking state of affairs," said Faith with a judgemental smack of her lips. "I don't know what father will ever think. But

I suppose we'll have to take the child in. Not for the whole summer, mind you."

Bernice went back to the kitchen, muttering to herself. "Poor youngster, with a cold-hearted crowd like that for a family. Poor little Sharon."


"You'll answer when spoken to, child."

Sharon felt the tug as Aunt Faith tightened the ribbons on her braids. "You're a McGrath, my girl, and we don't take a back seat."

Wincing, Sharon shut her eyes tight.

"Don't show me those red eyelashes of yours, Sharon O'Dea. You're just too shy altogether. Now, speak up!" Aunt Faith gave a last yank on the braids. "I'd say what you need is a sister or brother. Then you'd soon learn to join in."

Sharon dreamed of having a little sister, all sprinkled with freckles like herself. But there was little hope of that. For as long as she could remember, her parents had lived apart, sleeping in separate bedrooms. Mommy in a grand boudoir with a bay window overlooking the garden, Daddy in a back room, as if he were just a passing guest. More than one night, Sharon had been awakened, gone out into the hall and seen him sneaking up the stairs to the maid's room in the attic, *in his pyjamas*. In the mornings, she'd crack open his bedroom door and look in at his sleeping form, always checking to see if he was back in his own bed.

Out on the Cape, it was another big house full of plush furniture where adults swirled around her. Aunts and uncles came and went or stayed behind closed doors upstairs. But she had her ways of finding out about them. She'd wait until the coast was clear, then rifle through the pockets of the coats hanging in the front porch. Each one contained pieces of secrets—in grandfather's, a bottle of pills like the ones Mommy took; and in Aunt Faith's, a photo from the newspaper, of a girl receiving a singing prize at the Mercy Convent School.

On the long summer days, she roamed through the tall yellow grass in the field. Beyond the fence, she could hear the local youngsters laughing, fighting, negotiating their way with each other, a rough and tumble spontaneity she had never known.

One sunny morning, they called out to her, "Whataya doin' out in the field in a party frock? Aren't ya comin' out to play? We're goin' down to the frog marsh."

She turned her head away. Too shy to respond and not allowed outside the fence, there was no play and no frog marsh for Sharon.

But then she discovered Bernice. In the kitchen, in the rattle of dishes and the smell of carrot and turnip boiling away on the stove. Bernice lifted her red knuckles out of a pan of dishwater, blew a wisp of hair off her face and gave a big smile.

"Comin' in for a little visit, my darlin'?"

Sharon took a few hesitant steps in her patent leather shoes onto the kitchen canvas.

Bernice scooped her up in her long arms. "Aren't you a sweet girl."

At first, Sharon's little body stiffened on contact, but, gradually, she took to being in the warm cradle of Bernice's shoulder.

And it wasn't long before Bernice got the little girl talking.

Sharon sat on the high kitchen chair swinging her legs. Her family's secrets poured out of her, with all the trust in the world. "Daddy gets mad at Mommy and bangs his fist on the table."

Bernice egged the child on. "And what does your mommy do then?"

"Mommy goes to bed and cries, Daddy knocks on the door, Mommy screams…I get scared." Tears came to Sharon's eyes.

Bernice placed her finger on the little girl's lips. "Shh. Never you mind that now, darlin'." And that was the end of the housemaid's shameless prodding.

From then on, when Sharon was in the kitchen, Bernice and the little one spent their time laughing and singing. They recited rhymes and Bernice sang hymns about Jesus and salvation. Sharon, a convent girl, knew nothing of this joyful

Jesus. Bernice thumped the counter and tossed her head as she sang.

"Praise the Saviour, he's coming to save our souls."

And it wasn't long before Sharon was jumping and thumping, too.

"Oh, you're a grand little girl," said Bernice, filled to the brim with joy. "Those McGraths don't know what they're missing. Mind now, your Aunt Faith don't want you havin' a good time in here with me. Next thing we know, you'll be going to the prayer meetin's."

Now that she's out of the McGrath house, Bernice has time on her hands. She's clearing out her cottage, sweeping away useless bits and pieces of the past—her father's war memories, badges and buttons of Empire and glory. She picks up the photo that sits in a frame on the cup shelf in the kitchen—her mother, peeping out with an unsure look, thin lips, watery eyes.

Why did Dad have to dwell on her all his life? No wonder I've always been lonely. My mother gone and my father wrapped up in his own sadness.

She pushes open the door to the garret where her mother died. All those years, Dad kept the room with the blinds down, a few mementos sitting on the dusty dresser. She picks up a soft little prayer book and sits on the bed.

If only she'd lived, I wouldn't have been placed with the McGraths. Barely sixteen and frightened to death. And after all I did, rearing their poncy youngsters, what was I to them in the end? Just a forty-somethin', scuffin' around with a broom. I worked away in their private nooks. Knew the sound of this one's breathing, the way that one ruffled the sheets. I cooked their fancy meals, did their dirty work, kept secrets for those daughters bawling down tears in their bedrooms, even cleaned up the night that Faith had her baby out of wedlock…but they were too high and mighty to ever give me the time of day.

In the evenings, when the McGraths sat in the front room listening to the radio, Sharon twirled around the armchairs, looking into their faces. Who were they all? Grandmother, forever "sickly" in her room, with her flabby arms, negligees and slurred voice; grandfather, too frightening a figure to approach, bellowing out orders; and, of course, Aunt Faith, a stiff beanpole of a woman with anxious dark eyes, dark like a caravan gypsy in a storybook.

Occasionally, they surprised Sharon and paid a little attention to her.

"You know, you've got the McGrath in you," said grandfather, proprietorial. "Sharp-minded and determined." Sharon blushed. He turned to Aunt Faith and continued talking about Sharon, as if she weren't there. "A shy girl, with hardly a word in her mouth but watch out—she's nobody's little fool." He patted the child roughly on the arm.

She drew away.

*Irish Reels and Jigs* came on the radio.

"Do a little dance for us, now," said Aunt Faith. "They must teach you the Belfast Hornpipe at school."

Sharon was well practiced in the mincing steps and high kicking of the Irish jig, but spiteful, she clumped around the room, sabotaging the moment.

Aunt Faith turned the radio off.

"Sharp-minded and determined, no doubt. More like defiant, I'd say. Now get yourself straight up those stairs to bed, Sharon O'Dea."


As always, Sharon was put to bed too early for a summer's night. She lay awake and listened to the other children, still out shrieking across the fields.

It was Bernice who came to her bedside in the dusk. Sharon snuggled into the crook of the housemaid's arm, taking comfort in the smell of polish and soap that emanated from her.

Bernice was full of tales of ragged waifs and orphans lost in the woods. She fancied herself as a good yarn teller and took her time, lowering her voice to exaggerate ominous details: "A dark cloud passed over the sun…" or pausing in the scary parts: "Something moved in the bushes…out came the fairies…with their bright eyes and pointy noses…"

Transported, Sharon became that little girl wandering in a leafy glen, longing for a happy ending, finding disappointment.

After the story, Bernice tucked her in, covering her cheeks with kisses. And the little one let herself be cherished.

"Night, night," whispered Bernice.

In the silver morning, Sharon made the rounds with Bernice, to the wharf and the shops. She skipped along by the picket fences, running back to take Bernice's hand when she got too far ahead.

This poor little one's so timid, thought Bernice, relishing the motherly moment, she needs to be playing with other children. I knows it's not my place, but I'm going to take her down to the frog marsh.

Once at the marsh, Sharon shed her shyness and joined in the fun with the Cape Verde ruffians. She even fell into the swamp and got mud on her frock. Bernice pretended to scold. "Oh my! Look at the mess of you!" But really, it was an excuse to take the child in her arms, cajole her.

Next thing, Bernice decided to take Sharon up to her little cottage on Sunday afternoon, when naps were being taken at the McGrath house. The little girl's eyes were full of excitement as she and Bernice slipped out the back door and scurried up the path, looking back at the house, checking for a face in the window. No McGrath had ever set foot in Bernice's house. And rules had been laid down about where Sharon could go. Sharon was careful to clean the grass and mud off her shoes before entering the McGrath house for Sunday night supper. Nonetheless, the mouldy smell of Bernice's cottage lingered on her clothes. "There's a sniff of something foul in the house," said Aunt Faith as she served up the blancmange. "Bernice is falling down on the job again."

The next Sunday afternoon when Sharon came for her visit, Bernice fired up the oven and baked a pudding. They sat at the table in the warm kitchen. Sharon's cheeks went pink as she basked in the feeling of wholeness in the modest little cottage. Bernice chatted away, fussing over the little one. Bernice's father, Clyde, sat at the table, too. He was quiet, like Sharon. He ate his pudding and smiled at the little girl. Bernice could see that he was taking a liking to the child.

"Come out here, now, my dear," he said to Sharon, reaching for his cap, "till I shows ya something."

There's a spark in him, thought Bernice. Where did that ever come from?

Little Sharon trailed behind old Clyde. Bernice could hear her talking outside, her squeaky little voice all curiosity and delight. And Clyde chiming in with his few words: "Look at this bird's nest. Have you ever seen such wonder?"

After that, whenever Sharon came up to the cottage, Clyde took her out on a little foray. Bernice wasn't sure what to make of her sad old father befriending Sharon. "He never showed me no bird's nests when I was a youngster," she grumbled to herself.

"I might take the little one along berry picking," he said one afternoon in his gruff voice.

"Maybe not. You could be seen by the McGraths," objected Bernice.

"The McGraths don't be going up on the back hills," said Clyde. "And there's no harm to it."

Bernice shrugged. "I suppose not."

And off they went, the stooped old man holding a berry can and Sharon scrambling through the bushes with an empter. "Don't be running too hard, now," he chided. "You'll spill all the berries." Sharon gave him an impish little smile and kept running, braids flying loose of their ribbons. "Come back here," called Clyde, trying to keep his good nature. "Don't be wilful, my child."

Then one Sunday in August, near the end of summer, Clyde decided to take Sharon fishing on the lily pond up in the hills.

Out there on the pond, little Sharon and the old man fell into natural communion. They drifted along in their silence, listening to the chopping of the waves and the cry of the gulls making their sweeping loop inland from the harbour. "What's over there?" said Sharon, pointing to the lily pads. Clyde steered in so she could see the flowers up close. She was taken by the strange light they gave off, a pale yellow glow on the dark water. She reached out to pluck a lily.

"Sit still, my child." Clyde steadied the boat with a splash of the oar. A warm smile came to his hardened face. "They calls them flowers 'fairy lamps.' They're not for picking. This is where the fairies come to play."

"Can I be a fairy too?" said Sharon.

"Yes indeed," he said, his eyes watering, "A real dainty fairy, with all the magic."

Sharon was half scared to look into Clyde's ancient face with the wrinkles and stubby beard, but she took comfort in his careful manner. To a fault, he was gentle, but very firm about certain things.

"You mind yourself in this boat. They says this pond is so deep it reaches all the way down to the sea."

Sharon looked at the water, so black it gave no reflection of the surrounding hills.

"Don't you go leaning over," said Clyde. "This little boat will tip in a wink."


Bernice has finished her sweeping now. She looks out the window, down the valley that always made her father think such sad thoughts. She starts making supper, setting a single place for herself at the table.

Dad was a quiet old soul, but this place sure feels empty without him. He didn't mean no harm taking Sharon out on the pond. He was just happy to show her the hills. He was only trying to give the child a bit of love. Not that he ever gave me that much. But he put a smile on her face. Those McGraths don't care about how good we were to her.

Clyde and Sharon had been out on the pond all afternoon. The sun dipped behind the hills and a bite of chill came with the shade.

Sharon shivered. "I'm cold, Uncle Clyde. I want to go home."

"Alright," said the old man, "we'll get going." As they moved close to shore, Clyde whispered. "Look up, child, eagles on the high ledge."

Mother eagle stood guard on a spruce branch as her full-grown fledgling, perched on the rim of the nest, attempted to fly.

"I see them," shouted Sharon, pointing up at the cliff. "The bird's flapping his wings, he's going to take off."

"Shh, stay still, now, my girl, don't stir."

The eagle flew off. Sharon kept scanning the hills and the shore.

That's when she saw it. Something flitting through the long grass by the shore. With a start, she stood up and leaned out. "Look, Uncle Clyde, look over there!"

Water rushed straight in over the low gunnels.

"Get down, child, get down!"

They tilted.

In a panic, Clyde leaned the opposite way to right the boat but he jerked too hard.

And they went over.

Sharon saw him slide under, then felt the icy water up to her neck. She kicked her little feet as they taught the convent girls at the King George pool in town. And she got to shore.


Bernice padlocks the door of the cottage and heads down the pathway to the church, taking a passing look at the McGrath property—the clapboard mansion with an Irish name painted in willowy letters over the door—*Ard na Mara*.

I'm glad to be away from that crowd and their uppity non-sense. No wonder Sharon liked to be with us. But I never should have let poor Dad take her out in boat. He didn't know anything about looking after youngsters. The child said she saw a fairy flitting through the grass along the shore—must have been a fox or a rabbit. I never should have told her those stories. She could be excitable, that little one. Like a caged animal let out. It's her family's fault for never letting her have a good time. A child needs a bit of fun. Even heartless old Faith said that.

No doubt that Meredith got what she wanted. Her own child sent away to school, being reared by nuns, for God's sake. And that poor little girl so lonely.

Well, Missus is free as a bird now. All she got to do is eat chocolates all day.


The church is blazing with lights tonight.

"You lead us in a hymn now, Bernice," says the pastor. "We all want to hear you." Pastor Hewell, a monolith of a man, with a hook nose. Not much of a looker, but he's a widow, looking for a wife—he's up for grabs. Bernice has him in her sights. That would do just nicely. Put down the bucket and broom and become a pastor's wife, tossed off in suits and dresses and little hats.

People are talking. They all know what the pastor's after. Bernice is no beauty—big and awkward—but her Sunday dinners and dainty sweets are famous. She's been baking "melting moments" for the pastor, little finger cakes with soft icing that melts away like nectar on your tongue. He wants them on his tongue—he's getting ready to pop the question.

Bernice stands by the pastor and sings her head off.

"Jesus wipe away my sins."

# CARPENTER'S
# SECRET

MARY TAKES HER place at the table in the dining room. Sunlight streams through the bay windows.

"Lovely morning," she says to the two other guests, already sipping their coffee. They smile politely, introduce themselves—Carla and James, from Ontario.

"Is this your first trip to the island?" asks Mary, trying to sound flat and even, like them.

The wife replies, clearly the talkative one.

"Oh no, we come to Cape Verde often. And we always stay with Mrs. Dodge."

"You must really like it out here," says Mary, banally.

The wife unfolds her napkin, looks pleased with herself. "Actually, we're thinking of buying a house on the island. To get away from Toronto, the pollution, the traffic…"

Doesn't she know that's a conversation stopper? thinks Mary.


Before Mary came out to Cape Verde, her friend Barb had filled her in about the big controversy on the island.

"Emotions are running high," she'd said. "Cape Verders are up in arms about the old houses being sold off to outsiders. The island is divided. And it's bitter. I grew up on the Cape and I know what they're like out there. They're clinging to the past. Those houses are like shrines. They think the place is blessed. Some kind of foggy paradise. And now they have to go off the island to look for work and can't afford to keep up the old family homes. The locals are taking it hard."

"Here you go now, my dears." Mrs. Dodge plonks the classic B & B breakfast on the table: eggs, bacon and toasted homemade bread, served on flowery Victorian dishes, blueberry jam in little crystal jars with silver serving spoons.

She gives Mary a hard stare, as if warning her not to say anything unwelcoming. "That's a good thing for this community, people buying up the old abandoned houses. What else are you going do on an island like Cape Verde with the fishery gone?"

Mary turns to the taciturn mainland husband.

"These old houses are beautiful but they can need a lot of renovation."

He aligns his knife and fork carefully on the plate, then gives her an awkward little nod in agreement. But not a gig out of him.

Mary smiles to herself. He reminds her of Charlie, so shy and boyish, she always had to rescue him socially. At least she doesn't have to do that anymore.

Sure enough, Carla, the chatty wife jumps in. "You're right. Fixing up a house is going to be a challenge. But it's very exciting thinking about all the possibilities." She glances at her husband. "Isn't it, James?"

Another couple appears in the doorway. The wife is very done up for so early in the morning. Hoop earrings and a bright orange and yellow blouse over her ample bosom.

"Good morning!" she sings out to the room. She's lively, confident. Blond hair in a flip, pretty.

Her husband comes in behind her. Mary sits up and takes notice. Wow! Tall Dark And Handsome, he's got it down pat.

There's something exotic about him—toasty skin and fine features. Maybe a touch of Beothuk, Mi'kmaq? Must be a musician, artist of some kind. Not often you see a man with a ponytail out in Notre Dame Bay.

They sit down and the wife takes over the table. "I'm Judy and this is George. We came over on the night ferry. Mrs. Dodge hired George to tear down her old back porch and put on a new one. I'm just along for a little holiday. Can't let him be out here wining and dining with you crowd without me." She laughs at her own joke.

Mary's wondering about the handsome husband. Strong silent type? She throws a comment in his direction. "That's going to be a quite a job, pulling down that big old porch."

Judy makes several quick hand gestures to George, including the sign for house, fingertips touching in the shape of a pointed roof. Mary recognizes the sign language from her teaching days. George signs back, tapping his lips lightly with his thumb, his face animated, his gray-green eyes talking to Mary.

"George says old porches are full of carpenter's secrets. He's looking forward to the job."

Mary bypasses Judy and addresses George. "Carpenter's secret? Sounds intriguing, I'd like to see one of those."

Now the mainland wife gets in on the act. "Do you come out to the island often?" she asks, also directing her question to George.

He's a magnet, thinks Mary.

Judy is quick to answer. "George can't get enough of it out here. He does a lot of work on the island. This is where he grew up, see." She looks at him lovingly, like it's endearing of him to be from Cape Verde. "He's always looking for an excuse to jump on the ferry and cross the tickle…even though it's just a bit of old rock out in the middle of the bay."

George is signing to his wife, his face full of laughter.

"George says a Gander girl married to a Cape Verde boy goes up in the world. There's high culture out here." She laughs, a rich, happy chortle.

Mary is curious. They seem like the perfect couple. That woman's crazy about her husband. Will I ever go back to being like that with a man?

The way you were with your husband, the way you are with men now. Around the dinner table, Mary and her divorced friends have been over that ground.

"How can you not be bitter?" says Barb. "It's a hard old statistic—a certain percentage of men simply dump their long-time spouse for a new, younger model. It's so unfair. But that's the way it is. Men will wander."

Mary shrugs her shoulders, defeated. "I never saw it coming. I thought Charlie and I were still in love. I just can't get over it. I'm awake in the night, inventing dialogues, angry rants."

"Why don't you have a nice little affair with some guy to boost your ego?" says Doris. "I've been with a few men since the divorce. Nothing serious. Just for fun. And I've learned a lot about myself."

"Go on, Mary, get out there," says Linda. "Fifty's the new forty—you're still young and fit. And you're no shrinking violet."

Barb shakes her head. "Just don't go falling in love. I know what a romantic you can be. Too soon, too fast. That would only lead to more disappointment."

"Romance is the last thing on my mind right now," says Mary, her brown eyes intense. "I've decided to get away from St. John's. I'm going out hiking on Cape Verde Island. Have a good think about it all."

"That's perfect!" Doris exclaims. "You never know who you're going to meet out there. Some unsuspecting hiker. Don't pass up any chances."

"Chance encounters on that godforsaken island," says Barb, laughing. "Not a hope in hell."

"I'll just put on a fresh pot of coffee," says Mrs. Dodge.

Too UNSPEAKABLE for Words

No one's in a hurry to leave the breakfast table. It's all titillation—George and Judy gesturing, everybody laughing at George's jokes, teaspoons clinking in coffee cups, Mrs. Dodge coming and going.

George is having a big chat with the mainlanders now. Judy's fingers are going like knitting needles. She's enjoying herself, a warm pinkness creeping up her cleavage.

Carla-from-Toronto is elated, and her husband has even cracked a smile.

Mary is amused. There goes George, a deaf mute, fulfilling the mainlanders' image of the funny, friendly Newfoundlander. He sure knows how to play to the gallery.

"According to George, the island is multicultural," says Judy, with delight. "Every little settlement out here has its own ways, its own dialect."

"But surely, that culture's all gone now," interjects Carla in a nasal, know-it-all kind of way. "There's nothing left out here. This place has gone to seed."

George gets a dark look on his face. He sighs and starts signing.

Judy scrambles to deal with the change of tone. She shakes her head apologetically. "He says to tell you you're wrong. This island is brimming with life—lobster in the water under the rocks around the shore, partridgeberries thick on the barrens."

George motions to her to keep going.

"And it's not gone to seed. There's no end of beauty—the light on the hills in the morning, the coves at the bottom of the cliffs…"

"Yes, but you can't really make a living out here," says Carla, determined to keep speaking from her own sensibility. "I know it's a paradise when we're here in summer but how would you handle the isolation in winter?"

George crosses his hands on his chest, then taps his forehead with one finger.

"Okay, he says to tell you he loves this place," says Judy, lowering her voice in embarrassment, "more than any outsider could ever imagine."

Carla takes a gulp of coffee.

Mary's eyes meet George's. She looks away quickly.

My God, I'm pulled by him.


Mary's out walking the cliffs of Cape Verde. The day is sunny but windy and wild, waves crashing on rocks. She stops to take a long look at the light glistening on distant islands.

Glorious, breathtaking, bigger than me and my little troubles.

"Try to heal yourself," the therapist had said. "Open a new chapter, step away from that story."

But how to step away. It's embarrassing, really. Stereotypical. Classic B movie. True love betrayed. A fifty-year-old divorcee, jilted. Heartless husband remarried to a young thing with firm flesh, wrinkle-free face.

Sherrie. No flies on her. She moved into Charlie's life like a hurricane. And he flew right out of our marriage—our life of thirty years, ripped up from the roots. I wonder if that Sherrie feels guilty about being a husband stealer. Not likely, by the look of her at Pam's wedding. You'd think *she* was mother of the bride, hanging off Charlie's arm in the family photos, done up in a cheap, too-tight dress. And me, skinny and gaunt from hardly sleeping or eating for the past few months, trying to look serene and motherly in my tasteful linen shift.

Carla appears at a turn in the path. Out picking wildflowers, watching for whales.

"Did you hike all the way to the end of that rough trail?" she says. "Are you sure it's safe to go out on those cliff edges on your own?"

"Not to worry about me. I've got lots of experience on these old rocks," snaps Mary, impatient with the motherly concern, as if she needs guidance because she doesn't have a husband.

Carla changes the subject. "Oh! That George is right, you know. Cape Verde is gorgeous. We're so lucky. We're going to love it here. We're not supposed to say anything yet, but we've just bought that lovely old house out on the point. I know it's sad people have to sell their family property. But we're going to respect and look after it."

She looks at Mary, as if for approval.

"It's a tough old dilemma, having to sell an ancestral home," says Mary, not giving absolution. "How did you manage to get hold of that place? Prime location on the island. Sheltered by that gorgeous rock face. Facing out to the western sea."

Carla gets a dreamy look in her eye. "Oh, it's all thanks to Mrs. Dodge. Did you know she's got her real estate license? What an amazing woman! Besides running the B & B, she's busy selling houses."

That's not a B & B, thinks Mary, it's a trap.

"Apparently, the family that owned the house couldn't agree on whether to sell, but she convinced them to go ahead with the deal. It all happened in a whirlwind. I don't think the For Sale sign ever went up. Mrs. Dodge only gave us a few hours to make up our minds."

The dreamy look goes out of Carla's eyes.

"To be honest with you, I had a really rough time with my husband. He almost made us lose the deal. He thinks it was too hasty. James is the cautious type." She raises her eyebrows. "But I insisted we go ahead. It's a once in a lifetime opportunity! And Mrs. Dodge is even taking care of arrangements to get the place fixed up."

Barb had filled Mary in about Mabel Dodge. A real piece of goods. Came to the island from Grand Falls in her youth and married a widower from a merchant family. The old merchant died years ago. Once he was out of the way, she plugged into the new tourism, got her real estate license and started buying and selling houses. There were lots of beautiful old places available because the fishery was going down and people were leaving. She even managed to get hold of the McGrath mansion—with all its fancy fixings, it turned out to be the perfect B & B.

Mary had watched Mabel at breakfast. A short, heavy-set

woman, she'd ploughed around the mahogany table setting down the food, listening intently to the conversation and throwing in her own two cents whenever she could.

"That's all well and good, snug little coves and lobster traps," she'd flung at George. "But you can't live in the past. Cape Verde has become a tourist destination," she'd pronounced, "and that's that."


They've started ripping down the old porch at the B & B. An elaborate structure for a back porch, long and wide with a big pantry on one side and, on the other, a comfortable seating area with winged chairs, picture windows and a view of the hills. George has a helper, Clarence, a cousin of his who lives on the island. He's got George's good looks and strong build. And nice manner. The young man knows sign language. They're chatting away. There's lots of laughter as they nudge at the woodwork with their crowbars. The building site has become a centre of attraction. Everyone dropping by to say hello, see how the work is advancing.

Mary goes out there.

I shouldn't do this. I'm looking for trouble.

She props herself in the doorway of the porch. "I've come to see the carpenter's secret."

George is only too happy to show her. He points to the window frame. Clarence interprets. "George says a carpenter's secret is to make your work invisible. Disguise how you do things."

"Isn't that a form of cheating?" says Mary, openly flirtatious.

George flirts right back with a gorgeous smile. He signs to Clarence.

"For George, it's an art form," says Clarence, enjoying the banter. "Look at that window frame. You don't see joining and finishing like that anymore. All flush and smooth. We're going to save what we can of it. That's our grandfather's handy work. See, George and I come from a long line of Cape Verde builders."

George looks around the porch. Wooden crossbeams, flared mouldings, trim work on the windows and doors, hand-hewn banister on the worn steps leading into the house.

Mary sees love in his eyes. Thinks, I'm like a girl getting a crush. "Too bad you have to tear the porch down," she offers.

"No choice. It's the wood rot," explains Clarence. "Can't you smell it?"

George gets a wry look on his face and gestures.

"He says to tell you it's like a lot of things, beautiful on the surface but rotten underneath."

Carla's husband, James, comes by. A petite, stiff man, impeccably dressed in khaki safari clothes, he's a contrast to the two big jovial carpenters in overalls. He peppers them with questions, writing their answers down in a tiny notebook.

Mary notices his neat, tight, handwriting. I bet he's a stickler to deal with. I see what Carla means. She must have her work cut out convincing him to do things her way.

"George will make the new porch look exactly like the old one," says Clarence with a look of pride. "He can reproduce all those fixings."

James looks up from his notebook. "Well, I might be needing—"

"So this is where you're hiding, James." It's Mrs. Dodge, turning up sharpish out of nowhere. "I've got tea brewed for you in the kitchen." She gives Mary a pointed look. "And you can't spend all day standing around watching these workmen. You'll be covered in dust and dirt. Come in now, the two of you, and we'll sit to the table for a nice chat."

Feeling admonished, Mary goes along to the kitchen.


Mrs. Dodge pours the tea, then pulls up a chair next to James.

"As I told you the other day, best not to go talking too much about the house for the moment."

James removes his Tilley hat, displaying his baldness. "I was just thinking that these two carpenters—"

"Early days yet. No need for people like George and Clarence to know the details. We won't be hiring them for the renovation job at your place, you see."

"I don't see why not," says James.

Mary smiles to herself. *I see what's happening. Mabel's got a programme and James is not complying.*

Mrs. Dodge passes around a plate of warm scones and jam.

"You see, James, I've gone and hired some workmen from St. John's to fix up your house. Cape Verders get insulted about outsiders doing work out here. As I say, best not to mention anything."

"But George is a real heritage carpenter. Skilled and knowledgeable."

"So it's *heritage carpenter* he's calling himself now. I wouldn't get too drawn in by that *heritage* racket if I were you."

James pushes his chair away from the table. "I'm not *drawn in* by anything. I can see for myself the quality of his work. I'm going to insist that we hire him to do the restoration."

Mrs. Dodge wipes the nice look off her face and the friendly cup-of-tea moment turns on a dime. "That would be a breach of contract," she barks. She starts clearing the tea dishes. "You signed on the dotted line with what I arranged." She wipes the table vigorously. "There's no going back now."

James stands up. "Well, we'll have to see about that," he says, matching her bullheadedness with his own. "I'm not the pushover you might think I am." He leaves.

Mrs. Dodge turns to Mary. "Don't mind any of that now, my dear. These mainlanders come out here acting like they own the place. But really, they haven't got a clue. We have to let them know who's boss sometimes."

Mary gives Mabel a distracted nod. Her mind has already gone to George. If he's a heritage carpenter, why didn't Mabel offer him the job to renovate James and Carla's house?


Mary is the last to sit at the dinner table. The first thing she does is take a glance at George. He's not in the limelight tonight. Judy's keeping the chat going, all on her own. She's bonding with Carla.

"You'll have to come visit us in Gander. We have a split-level bungalow in the new subdivision."

Mary's trying not to look at George.

I wonder how he likes living in a bungalow in Gander. It's like any marriage, I suppose. He feeds off the good parts, puts up with the bad parts. She takes a quick glance at him. He has a way of listening, watching. He must be lip-reading.

"We'd love to visit you in Gander," gushes Carla, looking at James as if to say, "Join in and be enthusiastic." But he's sour, scowling with his thin lips.

Judy forges ahead. "We'll show you some hospitality, cook you a real Jiggs dinner. Gander is worth a visit—we have an aviation museum—Gander used to be the crossroads of the world, you know."

Mary digs in her mind to remember the sign for work. She interrupts the Gander conversation. "How's the demolition advancing?" she ventures, shaping one hand into a fist and tapping the other wrist.

George emits a little grunt and gives her a soft look.

James pipes up. "I've been watching the care they're taking with the job. George and Clarence are first-class woodworkers. Mabel Dodge is lucky to have them working on her house."

The kitchen door flings open. Mabel marches in. "Oh! I don't know about lucky. There's no shortage of good carpenters." She places a platter of whole baked cod on the table. "Workers come and workers go."

James opens his mouth to speak, but Carla squeezes his arm, shutting him down.

"Now, enjoy your meal," says Mabel, declaring the subject changed. "'Tis the milk of the sea I'm serving you tonight."

She puts her hand on George's big square shoulder. "You get that down ya. You need your nourishment. I want that porch demolished and rebuilt before the season ends."

George leans forward to escape her hand.

Silence around the table.

"By the way, everybody," says Judy, bringing the tone back to sunny and bouncy. "There's a dance over to the church hall tonight. A fifties revival. Live music. George and I love to dance. We should all go."

Carla picks up on the bounce. "Oh! that would be fun, wouldn't it, James?"

James is deadpan.

Mary's mind goes back to Charlie. He used to get in funks like that, refuse to answer. And I'd be like Carla, trying to keep cheerful, patch things up.

At the dance, the B & B group cluster in one corner, waiting for the music to start up. The local men, ruddy faces clean-shaven, muscular torsos in freshly ironed shirts, stand in the doorway smoking. The women sit on chairs lining the walls of the church hall.

"It's so quaint," says Carla. "Look at the women waiting to be invited to dance."

"Stop talking like that," snaps James, liquored up on his third rum and coke. "Don't you know it's insulting?"

Carla gives Mary a nervous smile. "Don't mind him, he's a little drunk. Maybe you and I should sit along the wall and see if someone will invite us to dance."

"George and I just love to dance," says Judy, repeating herself with her usual enthusiasm.

The band strikes up. The first song is a jive, "Wake up, Little Suzie." George and Judy hit the floor. He's the one with the artistry. He leads her around, swinging, pushing and sloshing. Light on his feet. Full of music. Mary can't keep her eyes off him.

"Very impressive," slurs James. "This guy is a miracle. How does he catch the rhythm if he can't hear the music?"

"I've read about this," says Mary. "It's the vibrations. George can sense them—the room is full of them, in the doors, the walls, the floor."

Mary's itching for a dance. She spots George's cousin Clarence standing in the corner with the single men and beckons him over.

"I'm sure you're a good dancer like your cousin," she says, hooking his arm and bringing him onto the dance floor. The band is playing "Your Cheatin' Heart." Clarence moves smoothly.

"Where did you learn to dance so well?" asks Mary, looking over Clarence's shoulder at George and Judy, clenched in their slow waltz.

"George taught me. He taught me everything I know."

"He's quite the man," says Mary, still taking in how George and Judy are moving in sync, hips touching.

All those years of dancing with Charlie. Familiar skin on familiar skin. I wonder what it would be like to dance close with George?

Judy catches Mary's eye. Flashes her a big happy smile.

Mary gives her a weak smile back. What am I doing? That's her husband for God's sake!

Another slow dance starts up—"You Always Hurt the One You Love."

James invites Judy to dance, whirling her off with exaggerated arm movements.

From across the room, George talks to Mary with his eyes. Then he signs to her—two fingers pointing down at an open palm. Mary nods in agreement. Over he comes and she finds herself waltzing in his arms.

He's a big man but his touch is light. It's excruciatingly slow, this dance. Mary starts talking nervously. "Cape Verde seems to be a real hotbed of dancers, everyone's up on their feet..." Then she catches herself, embarrassed. George winks at her and pulls her a smidgen closer. She lets herself slide into his deep, slow turns. Oh God! He really knows how to lead. Don't let anyone see how good this feels.

The song ends. George holds her for a minute. She can feel his heart beating. What now? she thinks. I don't want to let go. The next song is starting up. He gives her hand a tender squeeze, steps away and returns to his wife.

Judy's husband, thinks Mary. Judy's husband.

Intermission. Mary's eyes follow George and Clarence as they join the men in the corner. James trails along after them. The men pass the rum bottle. James is red-eyed and he's talking to the other two, intently, haranguing. Mary moves a little closer, but in the din of the hall, with people chatting and laughing, chairs scraping, she can't catch a snippet of what James is saying. Clarence is interpreting and George is nodding his head at James, smiling, indulging the drunkard. Then, suddenly, George goes sombre, pained, like he's just been told the worst news imaginable. He looks dramatic, a silent film character in distress. Clarence looks shaken too. He's explaining something to James. Over the noise, Mary hears James shout, "...that bitch Mabel Dodge."

Judy is with George now and they're signing away, hands flying. George is twitching and sighing. Clarence keeps patting George's shoulder.

Mary's tempted to go over there.

I wonder what's happened. Poor George! He's devastated. Barb was right—it's all drama out here on this god-forsaken island. Oh! for heaven's sake, stay out of this one, girl.

Mary's back at the B & B, perched in the rocker on the front veranda, glass of chardonnay in hand.

The night sky is laden with stars, moonbeams catching the tips of the waves out in the bay.

Keep looking at the bigness, she says to herself.

There's the squeak of the screen door opening.

It's Judy.

"George is gone to bed. Thought I'd join you."

As she sits down in the other rocker, her overly sweet perfume wafts over Mary.

"I admire you coming out here hiking on your own. I'd be lonely without George."

She pauses before asking the inevitable question: "Do you have a man in your life, my dear?"

"I'm divorced. Freshly."

"That's too bad. Big adjustment, I guess. No wonder you need time to yourself."

Mary pours Judy a glass of wine.

"Your husband seemed tired when we left the dance," she says, as casually as she can. "Must be working hard."

"George has a big sulk on tonight."

Mary is surprised by the sharing. "Did something go wrong today?"

"Ah! I wish he didn't take things so hard. It's that house those mainlanders bought here on the island. It actually belonged to George's Uncle, John Grimes. George loves that old place; it's full of childhood memories. His two cousins inherited the house, and planned on selling it. But they promised George they'd let him have first dibs. George has been scrambling to raise the down payment. But tonight he found out that Mabel Dodge convinced the two cousins to go ahead and sell the house to James and Carla—for a much higher price then George could ever pay, of course. You see, George misses out on stuff because of being deaf and dumb. People take advantage." Judy downs her wine. "He's hoppin' mad with those cousins. We don't need that old broken-down house, I keep telling him. But he gets so emotional. He says Mrs. Dodge is a real snake too. She never breathed a word to him about this. But I can see why she wouldn't. She's got a business to run. George has got it in for her. He's thinking about revenge. He can be the devil when he wants to, you know. I'd say he should keep on the good side of her. Sure, we've got our nice house in Gander…"

Mary is trying to hide her indignation. Poor George! All she can think about is her bloody bungalow in Gander. She interprets for him but wants to override his feelings. Cape Verde is his lifeblood and she couldn't care less!

"Well, I'm off to bed," says Judy. "With all the socializing, and now this big fuss tonight, me hands are worn out from talking. Himself is probably snoring it off by now. I'm sure this will all blow over by tomorrow."

Mary lies in bed.

It's all George now. He's chasing Charlie out of my mind. Am I that fickle? Maybe it's because I'm so lonely. And George must be lonely too. Walled in by silence. Depending on Judy to connect with the world. But the whole thing is ridiculous. Another classic B movie. The sensitive man with a wife who doesn't understand him. The wounded divorcee falling for a handsome green-eyed stranger. The cunning businesswoman pulling strings to make things go her way. The money-laden outsiders stealing the locals' heritage.

Through the wall comes Carla's voice, shrill.

"You're going to ruin everything, James."

"I never should have let you snowball me into this, Carla. I'll be damned if I honour the contract with that Mabel Dodge."

"What's wrong with you? Do you have some kind of thing for that George? And, anyway, we shouldn't get involved in local politics. Mabel has a lot of influence. We don't want to fall out with her. We might need her sometime."

"Forget Mabel. George is our man."

"I can't stand it when you're like this, James. I'd just as soon go back to Toronto."

Mary remembers those arguments. Charlie always stuck to his guns. If she didn't give in, there was no way out. In the heat of the moment, she'd feel like walking out of the marriage. Then she'd get over it and carry on, wounds and all.

Next morning at breakfast, James looks grey.

Carla has put on her red lipstick. And she's back on course. "I don't know how you manage, Mabel. This beautiful house, wood polished, silver shining. And so much home cooking, all so good."

"That's only the half of it," she replies, shooting a look at James. "I've got a lot of business going on the island, you know."

"George has something to announce," says Judy, in a

one-note drone. She closes her eyes, as if to disassociate herself from the message. George is impassive, letting her do all the work. "This will be his last day on the job. He'll remove the rest of the wood trim but he won't be finishing the demolition or building the new porch."

Mrs. Dodge folds her fat arms over her chest. "Well, I don't see why the paying guests should be party to this. And what's this new trend now, not honouring contracts?"

"I can't blame him," says James, out of a woolly head. "We'll be checking out of here ourselves, tomorrow morning. And for sure, we won't be using the St. John's contractors to renovate our house."

"But let's enjoy our last day," chirps Carla. "I've got a bottle of bubbly for tonight. It's our wedding anniversary. James and I were married 10 years ago today."

James gives a "not now" wave of the hand to Carla and turns to Judy. "Please tell George I'll be counting on him for the renovation. We can go over there this morning and I can give him an idea of our plans."

Judy fiddles with her napkin, lets out a sigh and makes a few signs to George.

"Let me bake a nice anniversary cake for tonight," booms out Mrs. Dodge, giving Carla a false smile.

"I'll help decorate it," says Judy, joining the women's cabal in a wobbly voice.

James beckons to George and mouths his words slowly, "Let's go find Clarence."

The two men leave the table.

Judy jumps up. "I'd better see what George is up to, I suppose." She rushes out the door, high heels clicking on the hardwood floor.

"I'm ever so sorry, Mabel," says Carla. "My husband can be very difficult."

"Not to worry," says Mabel with a menacing look. "It's all George's fault. The only reason he's offering to help your James with the house renovation is to get back at me. George does some building and restoration, but he's only a small-time carpenter.

Take it from me, he's not equipped to take on a big renovation like that, especially with the grand plans you and James have, marble bathrooms and all." Mabel pats Carla's arm. "I know what can and can't be done out here. Your husband will be back, cap in hand, looking for those St. John's contractors. You mind my words."

Before dinner Mary pours herself a glass of wine and heads for the front veranda. Another long gaze out over the miraculous bay.

Through the open kitchen window she hears Judy and Mrs. Dodge chatting as they decorate the anniversary cake.

"We'd better add some more icing to stabilize that plastic bride and groom," says Mrs. Dodge, with a wicked chuckle. "They remind me of Carla and that husband of hers. About to topple over."

"George is not coming back to Gander with me tomorrow," says Judy in that way she has of spilling things out. "He's staying on the island to help James with the Grimes house."

"I'd say he's getting way in over his head with that project. And he should know better than get involved with the likes of that James," says Mabel. "A hothead if I ever saw one."

"Maybe after that he'll come back here to build your porch," says Judy. "When the dust settles."

That's out and out betrayal! Mary whispers to herself.

The screen door to the veranda opens slowly. It's George. He's finished work for the day, has showered and changed. He motions to the other chair, inviting himself to sit down. Mary notices the grey flecks running through his dark hair into his ponytail. She takes a gulp of wine.

I'm nervous like a teenager. How can I talk to him?

But he takes over, slips a notebook out of his shirt pocket and writes,

*You're a good dancer*
Mary writes back,
*You too*

He points out to sea—the bank of dark storm clouds sitting on the horizon. Mary points at the new moon, a faint slither, low in the sky. They start a pointing game—the lean in the crabapple tree shading the house, the irises pushing through the rocks, the fading imprint of a galloping horse on the door of the old rotting shed…

Then a pause.

George emits a little moan, takes her hand.

Judy's husband, thinks Mary, Judy's husband…

# LEARNING TO TANGO

SPRING CAME EARLY and blessedly warm. Icebergs floated past the Narrows on a sunny sea, ancient lilacs in uphill backyards on the South Side bloomed well before their time, and the French fleet came to town.

They arrived on a glorious Sunday morning—six steel hulks of warships, all flags flying—and docked three abreast, right in front of Bowring's.

I was nineteen and determined to learn French and go live in the south of France under the palm trees, where the sea is as warm as bathwater and sophisticated people sit around in cafes all the time. My plan was strategic. I was meticulous with my conjugations and read every last word the professors assigned me—thick books about romantic heroes in capes pursuing happiness, or little existential novels about individuals who could see no meaning to life.

My best friend, Jennifer, was majoring in French too. But Jennifer was far from being a good student. She didn't practice her nasal sounds in front of the mirror or ever actually read her way through a Balzac novel. The single driving force in her life was getting away from her parents. French was her ticket off the island and out of the Hearn home, a row house on the slope of the hill behind the Basilica, where her family had been planted for generations.

"It's just not fair," she'd moan to the other girls. "I don't get to go anywhere. All they want is for me to stay on the hill and have babies, go to Mass on Sundays and be buried in the Belvedere cemetery when I die." She'd get an angry little flush on her red-headed white skin. "They can go right ahead and disown me if they want. I swear, I'm not going to stay on the hill."

My parents, on the other hand, had been away, on bus tours of Europe, and considered themselves a cut above families like the Hearns, who had never been anywhere. Mom and Dad were all for the idea of me going off to Europe when I got my B.A., though Britain would have been preferable over France. And they certainly weren't sure about letting me attend a "do" on a French ship with the "university crowd" and "all those Frenchmen."

"But Mom, they're officers," I pleaded. "We're going to practice our French. Everyone's going, even Glenda Moores."

Glenda Moores, the minister's daughter, lent a faint stamp of approval to the event. So they finally agreed to let me go, "As long as the professors are there to supervise."

In those days, the professors in the French Department were mostly British and constituted in themselves a fairly exotic species. Quite a few of them had actually been to France. And they had beards and wore sandals with socks, even in the dead of a Newfoundland winter. When you saw them around town, you wondered how and why they ever got here, but if you saw them teaching, you knew they had a mission, to pass on knowledge about alexandrines, the division of literature into centuries, and the importance of nothingness—*le néant*.

I sat in the front row, searching their faces, absorbing the British highlights of French culture with every fibre of my being. And in the evenings, I poured over the French centuries in my little bedroom at the back of my parents' bungalow on Forest

Road. Try as I would, I could never fathom nothingness. It didn't make sense in a place like St. John's, where life is curious and intense, full of eye contact and quirkish remarks from strangers. There might be despair all around you, but not nothingness—far from it.

The invitation to a dinner on the ship led to days of frenzied preparation. The girls laid out a detailed plan—who was to link up with whom, what to wear, what to say. I even invented possible dialogues, going over and over them in my head and immersing myself in a complete fantasy about which officer I would fall in love with and which part of France I was going to be invited to.

Of course, Jennifer's parents were to be kept completely in the dark about the whole thing. Mr. Hearn was well-known around town. He held an office in the Knights of Columbus and was planning to run in the municipal elections. On Thursday nights after supper, he put on his good suit and, smelling of aftershave and a bit red in the face from taking a bath, went off to the K of C meeting. No daughter of Francis Hearn could ever be seen going on boats in the harbour. Last year, Jennifer had been a debutante and had her picture in *The Daily News* in a formal white gown. The dress was chaste and revealed nothing of her saucy little pointed breasts but she still managed to look defiant, standing in front of the gilt-edged mirror over the fireplace. She had none of the sweetness of the other debutantes, posing primly in stiff dresses and elbow-length evening gloves.

Jennifer was well-practiced at sneaking out to forbidden places, but lately her style had been cramped by the return of her sister Theresa—"Treese" as they called her—from the convent. Treese had joined the stream of nuns leaving the Orders at the dawn of the new progressive age and now she was back in the family fold. The Hearns expected Jennifer to take Theresa, who was three years older in age, but nowhere near that in experience, everywhere she went. Treese's very presence was enough to ruin a night out for the girls. She still had this holy, plain way about her that made you feel like you had to mind your mouth and be extra good. If she was spoken to, particularly by a male, she'd drop her eyes, and she only ever gave one-word answers in a whisper of a voice. But if there was no Treese, there was no Jennifer, and Jennifer, with all her high spirits, had to be one of the group on the ship. So Treese was sworn to secrecy and came along—Jennifer's millstone at the French dinner.

It was the warmest night yet. A dream of a night. The whole town was outside. Couples courted on Signal Hill with car windows down, and people lingered on kitchen chairs in their front doorways. Even the summer inchworms, thinking it was July, had come to life, squirming in the trees and dropping onto sidewalks.

The wharf was crowded with strollers and onlookers who watched curiously as the girls from the French Department arrived at the ship, done up to the nines in planned outfits and dowsed in "Evening in Paris" perfume. Teetering on the narrowest of high heels, we made our difficult ascent up the gangplank, so excited and nervous we almost tripped onto the waiting officers, impressive and cool in full uniform.

So warm was it that aperitifs were served outside on the deck. The professors—a few with wives, but most single—had turned up early. Already on their second drink, they were more convivial than any of their students had ever imagined they could be. They sat there sipping *pastis*, staring at the oil tanks and shacks on the South Side hills as if they were on some yacht in Cannes. It was a rare sweet night, so calm you could hear the boys shouting up on the hills. The harbour water was barely moving, just swirling in slow, luxurious circles.

At first, hard pressed to know how to behave, the girls squirmed on squeaky folding chairs while the Frenchmen hovered around, smiling and chatting away as if this type of event happened every day in St. John's harbour. But it wasn't long before fingers began flipping through pocket-size dictionaries that fit into little evening purses. There was giggling and whispering and consultation: "How do you say *I'm not going steady?*" or "My God, I can't understand a word he's saying but he's gorgeous!"

After a *pastis* or two on empty stomachs, we had to manoeuvre our way down the steep stair ladders and narrow passageways to the dining room, where boy-girl seating at the table was promptly arranged by the officers.

Somehow, I managed to find myself seated between the only two "old" men in the room. On one side was my linguistics professor, a neat, quiet Englishman with gold-rim glasses who was already undergoing a change in personality from the drink; on the other side sat the "Commandant," the ship's captain, a grisly little man who smelled of garlic and *Gauloises* and was patently lecherous in the way he ran his hand across the nape of your neck. All the girls had been avoiding him, and the chair on his right side was the last remaining empty. Suddenly, he noticed that ex-nun Theresa was lingering in the doorway, waiting to be seated—a lamb for the slaughter. He jumped up gallantly, put his glad arm around the waistband of her blue serge skirt where the white blouse tucked in, and swept her to the table. She sat down with what looked like terror in her eyes.

Poor Treese had been long left to her own devices by Jennifer, who was already way out of control on the funny tasting liquor that made your lips go numb. And, truly, the quality of her French was the last thing on her mind. She just flirted and flitted around, leaning across our linguistics professor, James Jenkins, to ask me for translations and inventing words by just adding an é to English verbs. *J'ai trippé, j'ai mové.*

Glenda Moores, the minister's daughter, had made a big splash. Just recently crowned "Miss Freshette," she was stunning in her reigning queen outfit, a shiny peach-coloured dress. But Glenda had batted off all advances from the officers. Now, she sat in isolation at the end of the table, icy and imperious, twiddling the ends of her Twiggy-straight blond hair. The girls all knew her game—French practice was only an excuse to get out of the house. Gorgeous Glenda had other fish to fry.

"What time is it?" she kept asking in her sharp little voice. "I have to get out of here soon."

For the rest of the girls, the night on the ship was still young. They lapped up the officers' lavish attention and played the perfect guests, swallowing the funny animal organs served for dinner and making exclamations with rising and falling intonation, straight off the "French Made Easy" tapes in the language lab: *Que c'est bon! C'est délicieux! Qu'est-ce que c'est?*

Dinner was a long drawn out affair, with floods of wine. By now, male hands were wandering onto bare legs sticking out of mini-skirts and girls were looking across the table at each other with big eyes. Inevitably, it got to the point where it was time for a conference in the bathroom. The toilet was hidden behind a labyrinth of decks and clunky steel doors, and civilians were not allowed to walk around the ship unaccompanied. So there was no getting away from the men. A line of sailors waited dutifully outside the bathroom while, inside, the girls shrieked and howled and exchanged advice on just how far they should go. On the way back to the dining room, a few of them experienced their first French kiss, pinned up against chimneys, in the smell of bilge water and oil.

But I was back at the table with Professor Jenkins, missing out on the whole battle plan. Apart from Miss Freshette, I was the only one of the girls not by now paired off with a Frenchman. And there was nothing at all French about James Jenkins, who was the most delicate and cultivated of Englishmen. I kept looking around at the other girls with their doting Latin officers. I wasn't even getting a chance to practice my French—me, the ringleader, who knew the past subjunctive and where to put the pronouns in the negative imperative. The fact was, to my surprise, I was finding myself quite taken by the soft-spoken Englishman with the watery sensitivity in his eyes. The wine was making him just a little sentimental, and I was soon abandoning the Eiffel Tower and the Champs-Elysées for cottages in Dorset and lochs in the Scottish Highlands.

Around the large oval table that almost filled the dining room, the noise level was reaching a deafening pitch. It was a real party now, with big outbursts of laughter and strangers teasing and joking like they'd known each other for years. Between courses, people got up and milled around. The room was humming.

Only the captain and Theresa remained seated, at the end of the table, oblivious in deep *tête à tête*. Treese was well over her shyness. Nodding like she meant business, she was doing all the talking, expounding and explaining at great length in her Irish-sounding convent-taught French. The captain was keeping his hands to himself, but he leaned his body as close to her as he dared, and filled her glass after every sip. At one point, I heard him tell her that she was *une femme magnifique*. Theresa smiled, the biggest smile of her life.

After dinner, the group moved on to the lounge next door, a long, narrow room with couches and a line of little tables and chairs, like in a bar. At that point, a few girls—the weak of heart and the uncommitted, including Glenda Moores, who had curled her lips and turned up her nose at everything—left the ship.

The rest of us stayed on and learned to tango in clouds of Gauloise smoke. Scratchy 78s filled the room with the nasal voice of Edith Piaf. I was dancing rather close to Professor Jenkins. He smelled like Yardley soap: clean and proper. Clearly, he didn't know how to tango, but his hand was squeezing my bare shoulder tenderly. Across the smoky room, I could see Theresa and the captain, sitting in a darkened corner, their two heads touching. The others were all dancing and dancing. The Frenchmen, shorter and slighter than Newfoundland men, were twirling the girls. Even Inge Wesche, the broad-shouldered German exchange student who towered over them all, was being swung around and around to this wonderful accordion music that wasn't Irish, and the room smelled of this flowery aftershave that wasn't Old Spice.

The girls were so seriously paired off now that they stopped consulting each other for translation or protection. They just soaked up all the compliments and declarations of love, smoked the cigarettes lit for them and drank the champagne passed around in long thin glasses. Before long, there was necking going on, right in the room. Some of the girls stayed out of harm's way by keeping their mates dancing, arms straight out, head up, like they'd seen on *The Ed Sullivan Show*. Jennifer, who was wearing a velvet party dress her mother had made her for Christmas, finally reached her limit with the champagne and had to be taken out on the deck, where she was sick all down the dress and over the side of the ship.

By now, I was in earnest poetic conversation with Professor Jenkins, but it crossed my mind that the two Hearn sisters had gone way beyond their curfew. The party was continuing well into the black of night. I took a quick, concerned glance around for Treese, but she and the captain had disappeared altogether.

Someone put on Spanish dance music, loud, and shouted, "Gypsy Tango!" Everyone, even Professor Jenkins, jumped up with shrieks of *Ole!* amidst flailing flamenco arms and stomping feet. The room was so hot the sailors were dancing in their shirtsleeves, revealing their hairy Mediterranean-tanned forearms. All the portholes had been opened onto the soft night, but there still wasn't a breath of wind outside, and not even a whiff came off the Atlantic to penetrate the close little lounge that, by now, none of the girls wanted to leave, ever.

At this moment, at the very height of it all, Mr. Hearn made his big burly appearance in the doorway, holding a sickly, mortified Jennifer by the arm. She was white and weak and the satin bow on her bodice was hanging wet and wrinkled down the front of her dress. When I caught sight of him, the romance of the night drained straight out of me. I sprang back from Professor Jenkins and worked my way across the room through the wild dancers until I stood before Mr. Hearn. He looked stunned. And livid. His big torso was swelling up and the threat of violence was coming off him.

"Who allowed the like of this to be going on?" he shouted over the tango accordions. "I'm going to report the whole lot of you to the university. I'll have this written up in *The Evening Telegram!*" He looked around the roomful of clinched couples who still hadn't noticed his arrival and bellowed even louder over the din, "And where in Holy Name is Theresa?"

But he didn't wait for an answer, just wrenched Jennifer's arm hard and marched out, brushing past the stretched-out hand of one of the officers who had just come over to greet him, all smiles and Gallic charm.

A few days later, the fleet sailed out as scheduled, and, within hours, the June fog that everyone hoped might stay away this year rolled in through the Narrows, thick and cold.

For a long time after, the girls lived in a state of lovesick flotation. They re-told stories of how they tripped the light fantastic with the French officers, enlarging and prolonging the ecstasy whenever they got a chance. But I was left with nothing but the reality of Professor Jenkins, for whom the champagne had worn off, entirely. When I tried to look at him, he got frantically busy with his papers, and whenever he spoke to me, he was wildly abstract, making it clear that anything but morphemes was out of bounds.

The following year, when the rest of us were moving on to blue jeans, hippiedom and mainland universities—and Jennifer was settling into the typist job her father had found her in the Confederation Building—Theresa married her French captain in a full ceremony at the Basilica. Then she went away to live in a white villa on the Mediterranean. And every year, she brought her little French babies home to the Hearn house, in June, when, God willing, the lilacs were blooming on the South Side Hills.

# THE SWEETEST
# MEADOWS

BARD'S COVE IS empty of people now, full of presence and nothing: fallen-in houses, leftover doorways, chips of china cups, the sole of a child's shoe. The turnip gardens have long grown over, doorsteps sunken into the earth.

Jamie stands on the hill, taking a sweep of the place—brook, meadows, pond, woods, cliffs, rocky beach, deep harbour.

Once I thought I'd have a life here: all the hard work, out on the water, up in the woods, people so close to each other, the endless round of helping out, the visits, the church-going, the loving, the hating. But I turned my back on it. And now look at the place—abandoned.

Dad never lived to see resettlement. He would have held fast, refused to leave. He spent all his days here, and his father before him. Poppy loved the cove, his little haven in the fold of the hills. He was a Bard's Cove man, for sure. And Dad too, in his harsh way, he belonged here, knew every shoal, every current, every switch of the wind.

I should have come home to see him before he died, found a way to forgive. But I know I'm as stubborn as he was. Old Reg, always at the helm, always so stern.

Reg called young Jamie into the shed and banged the door shut. "I saw you talking to that Millie Parsons. Don't you dare go near her again. They say she's got a reputation for being loose." He scowled, with a look of disgust that accompanies any talk of the flesh. "You keep yourself to yourself. You mind your bobber, James Cotter." Then he turned his back and tightened up his shoulders.

Jamie flinches, still feeling the edge of his father's sharp tongue. No wonder I left. How was a I supposed to grow up and make my way in that vice grip? It was always the keeping of order. You couldn't live. You had to stay clear of living.

I was just a lanky teenager, for God's sake. Trying to act like a man.

Millie wasn't from this part of the shore. She'd come down from Trinity for the summer to help her Aunt Becky Parsons with the newborn. People in Bard's Cove thought she was a real character, with her lively ways and her organizing events—Sunday picnics with youngsters running around, singalongs in the summer nights. Some said she was too much of a character, entirely, for a schoolteacher.

The first time he ran into Millie was out on the path. She wasn't alone. Her aunt and a couple of little ones were along, gathering blasty boughs for a bonfire. He'd heard her laughing as he came through the woods. He stepped into the clearing, and there she was, standing in a circle of sunlight, a load of boughs in her arms and strands of her black hair blown across her face. He stayed to help, glancing at her when he got a chance. Then, when she turned around and got down on her haunches, he took in the sight of her, following the movement of her body under her dress, the spread of her back and the curve of her wide hips. She knew he was looking, and as she stood up, flicking her hair off her face, she glanced in his direction.

There was a high wind that early spring day, banks of clouds racing through the sky, bursts of white sunlight on the new woods. The little ones were hanging off her skirts and running around her, and all the while she was laughing and indulging them with a lightness of heart that drew him to her.

A few days later he ran into Millie again. She was out strolling the baby, down by the wharf. A group of admirers had gathered around her—young teenage girls, all chatting, excited by her life force. Jamie hung around the edges of her circle. The girls turned to include him.

"Don't you want to talk to the women, now?" said Dulcie Poole, all flirty in her summer frock. But Jamie had no interest in Dulcie or any of those girls. He was fixed on Millie, already doting on her every trait: the freckles in the hollow of her neck, her slightly lazy left eye that made you wonder if she was really looking at you, and even the faint smell of sour baby's milk she had about her.

Finally, on the first warm day of summer, she acknowledged him. He was lingering by the fence in her aunt's laneway. She tapped on the kitchen window, motioning for him to come in. She was home alone. He sat in the kitchen, hardly daring to raise his eyes, but, slowly, she brought him around, reassuring him with that cheerful way she had of taking charge.

"Uncle George is down on the Labrador and we got no man in the house. You're good an' handy. You could help us out, if that father of yours would let you."

Jamie rubbed the back of his neck. She'd mentioned his father so casually.

"Now don't go getting all serious on me, young James. I know Reg is a hard ticket, but he can't be as bad as all that." She unbuttoned her sweater. "Getting hot in here with the stove going and the kettle steaming."

Jamie stared at the bulk of her breasts in the flowery dress. She gave him a knowing smile. "Could you shimmy up that old warped window for me while I run upstairs?"

He was only too glad to put himself to work.

A few minutes later she called down over the banister. "Why don't you come on up here for a minute?"

He knew full well to go no further than the cup of tea. Millie called out again, drawing him up the stairs. And he went, stepping lightly as if someone in the cove might hear him, his tall frame filling the tiny stairwell.

She was in the back bedroom, standing naked, heavy white breasts swelling with blue veins around big puckered nipples.

"I know what you're after," she said with a wink. "Come here now, my boy, your time has come." And she led him to the unmade bed, where he lay with her in that stuffy little room, in the smell of must from the old walls and the musky smell of himself and Millie, wrapping her legs around his oily work pants.

When she finally released him, he got straight up and made a thundering dash down the stairs, reeling out the kitchen door, catching the tail of his shirt on the thorns of the rose bush by the gate.


Jamie follows the path down the hill to where the Bard's Cove houses once stood, all clustered around the curve of the bay. He stops in front of the pile of rotting wood that used to be Becky Parson's house. Little pink flowers poke through the boards and the rusty bed springs.

Hardy roses, he thinks, all those years, all that weather, and look at that thorny bramble, still alive. He picks a rose and smells its perfume. So potent, like a keepsake. His mind goes to his mother. Poor Mom treasured her keepsakes—dried flowers, old buttons, bits of material. She had her secret longings, did Mom, wanting to go back to her younger years, before she married. When she'd get lonely for the past, she'd hold a piece of lavender-scented lace in her hand, looking for comfort.


"Pay attention to what you're up to, my son," chastised Old Reg, "you're going to let that net slip." They'd been out in boat since the crack of dawn, setting traps, but Jamie's mind was elsewhere.

It was all Millie now. For the last few weeks, in the long summer evenings, he'd been going faithfully to find her in the woods or the back meadows. Jamie, who'd hardly ever kissed a girl, had given himself over, completely, to this woman with the smooth skin always warm, even hot to the touch. He couldn't stop thinking about her—no matter where he was, fishing with Dad, home at the kitchen table with Mom, he kept reliving the feel of her, out there in the night, under a sky full of stars.

They planned their trysts around the comings and goings of people in the cove—who went up in what woods and what patch they went to. And all summer long, they got away with it. Only once were they surprised—by Millie's brood of nieces and nephews, a wild bunch of youngsters chasing through the bushes. The lovers hid behind the alders, Jamie stricken with fear, Millie full of silent laughter, her dimples deep in her big cheeks.

"Where do you be going these evenings?"

Jamie's mother had noticed a change in him. His bony adolescence was filling out. In the way he stood in the doorway or picked up his teacup or took off his cap, he was taking on the look of a man. But there was no doubt he was worried about something. She would find him standing alone in the upstairs hall window, looking out to the islands in the bay, as they loomed up and disappeared in the fog and the light. Poppy Cotter had put in this lookout window when he built the house.

Jamie looks out the bay—it had always been Poppy's favourite view, the sheep islands with their cliffs and tufts of grass.

Dad used to make fun of Poppy's special window. How it sat crooked in its frame and was drafty to stand in. "Your Pop's just an old dreamer," he'd say with that scowl of his. "Putting a foolish thing like that on a house."

Poppy never let me down, thinks Jamie. Always there with a kind word after Dad walloped me. "Come over 'ere, my child, take no mind, 'e can't 'elp 'imself."

Funny, I can still hear him, his accent—peculiar to that shore, and then again to that cove. A voice from another age, long gone from the earth.

Oh well, thinks Jamie. They've all become ghosts now, like the old spectres people used to see in the woods, or hanging around the cove, along the picket fences, in the attics, the sheds and stores and on the wharves.


Jamie was having daydreams, of himself and Millie taking their vows in the little church up the path. Millie had him trapped, caught in his urges to touch her, get inside her. Minutes after his shuddering satiation, he'd want her again. He needed to marry her, get rid of the feeling that he was doing something wrong. He was determined to propose, but he could never find the right moment. It was always jokes, good times and teasing with her.

"How can you go fishing with that skinny frame of yours," she'd say. "Sure, you can hardly lift a rope."

How often he sat folded in on himself while she moved through conversations, sweeping and swooping like a bat, never allowing a feeling or a thought to take form.


As the summer wore on, Jamie slowly came to realize that his mother too, was drawn to Millie.

One Sunday morning, as the cove people walked the pathway to church, Millie hooked on to his mother's slender arm.

"You're as smart as any teacher I've ever met, Virginia. Why don't you apply for the training? Then you could teach at the school here in the cove."

Virginia was a silent woman, always in the background, watching for her husband's nasty streak. But Jamie could see she was flattered, awakened by Millie's life-giving talk. There was a spring to her step and a girlishness in her voice he didn't recognize.

"Oh no, my dear, I can't be leaving my husband alone to go off for training," she said, bashful, but titillated. She looked at Millie with admiration. "You're so lucky, you've been to Boston. I've never been anywhere. When I finished school, I was supposed to get a church scholarship to go away for teacher training, but it never came through."

Jamie stayed behind with the men, but his eyes never left Millie. He watched her easy manner with his mother, all sympathy and interest. She kept her talking all the way back from church. Then she left her with a well-placed remark so they could pick up on the same note next time: "I'm telling you Virginia, you'd make a wonderful teacher. There's no doubt about it."

Mom was Jamie's rock of love. It pained him to deceive her. But he couldn't stop.


One Sunday in August, Mom decided to have Millie over for tea, a rare event in that house. She even went so far as to get the white tablecloth out of the trunk and spread it on the kitchen table, still smelling of mothballs. Millie came with all her boisterousness, full of church talk and compliments for Virginia.

Jamie could barely choke down the cake crumbs. He was seeing the cheat in Millie, hearing the falseness in her voice. Reg seemed to notice something too. He stayed at the table through the whole visit, through the tinkling teacups and women's talk he normally fled.


Summer drew to an end. Millie was due to go back to Trinity. And Jamie still hadn't proposed. The days were getting shorter, and as the berries ripened, groups of pickers forced the lovers out of their meeting spots. That's how they happened to be out on the point that day, way out where it reaches into the bay.

As they lay on the grass in the late afternoon, Jamie finally spoke up: "Millie, we can't go on like this. I want us to get married, be man and wife, like we should." He described the life they would have together in a house he would build, right down to the fancy woodwork around the front windows. Millie remained placid, wordless. His proposal became a plea, his throat dry.

"No more hidin' in the woods, now Millie. Marry me and we'll settle down in the cove. You could go school teachin' here."

She answered in a voice as straight as a dart.

"You didn't think for a second I'd ever stay on this shore. As soon as my chance comes to go back to my cousin's in Boston, I'll be gone." She slapped him jokingly on the shoulder to emphasize gone. She turned away. "It's getting cold, and the fog's moving up the bay," she said, picking up her clothes.

It was at that moment they were seen.

Down below the cliff in their boat stood Wilf and John White, two old bachelor brothers from the cove. Harsh judges. They gaped in disbelief and called out insults while the boat pitched in the swell.

"Get out of there with your shameful dirt and filth, bringing disgrace to this cove."

Millie scrambled to put her bare breasts back into the corset. For years after, versions of that vision were repeated in Bard's Cove—buxom Millie, naked in the grass.

They trudged back through the bog, their shoes sucked into wet clumps of forget-me-nots. Millie ploughed ahead and turned around only once to snap at Jamie, her lazy eye flickering. "It's your fault we got caught. All because of your nonsense, wanting to come out here to see the view."

Jamie's mother and father were waiting stony-faced in the kitchen. Wilf White had moored his boat and gone straight to their door with the news. It was silence overlaying silence in the house. In his mother's eyes, Jamie saw the hurt of betrayal and maybe a tinge of envy—a faint light of her long-forgotten girlishness. Reg was surprised at his son's prowess and gave him a rare look in the face, as if to see what he had never noticed all these years.

That night was the first true night of fall. The wind had come up and darkness was closing in early. Jamie could hear his mother in the kitchen, putting the kettle on.

"Come in here now, my son," she called to him in a pained voice. "Your father's gone out and I want to talk to you." But he couldn't bear to confront her. He slipped out the back door, closing the storm flap with meticulous care. Then he made his way along the path, feeling the weight of shame sitting on his shoulders.

When he got to the church, he stopped by the fancy iron-work gate, built by the men of the cove for the boys lost in France. Everybody's son, sacred ground. On an arch over the entrance: "HOLY HOLY HOLY." Words he'd never understood. As he stood there, he heard a sound, faint like a bird's call, but definitely the sound of Millie in her ecstasy. His heart pounding, he opened the gate and tiptoed through the graveyard, around the church to the sea-facing side where the wind was coming straight in. As the cold blast of air slapped him in the face, he took in the sight of his father and Millie in a clasp, against the white clapboards.

All the next day, Jamie stood looking out Poppy's window. By the time the sun had dipped behind the cliffs, he'd made up his mind.

He was leaving.


The clapboards are warped and rotting now but the little Bard's Cove church still stands, its stained glass windows with cranberry squares dancing in their crooked frames.

But this part of the shore remains empty, the hills thick with trees that end in a wavy line bordering meadows, flowery meadows rolling out to the edge of the cliff.

Jamie stands in a bank of buttercups, their waxy disks swaying on long stems in the July morning.

"The sweetest meadows in the universe," he says to himself.

# "THE ONE I GOT"

EMILY STOOD BY the church, watching the coastal boat navigate back down the inlet. There was one thought on her mind.

I should have told Mom.

It was July. All up and down the hills, banks of daisies rolled in waves as the wind swept through them. When the church bell started to ring, the men on the wharf, two boys in a dory, a woman at her clothesline, all turned their heads and looked. The steady ding ding of the tiny bell echoed off the cliffs. Patrick and Emily were to be married at this moment in this place.

"Mom will never forgive me for eloping, Paddy," Emily had protested, but only weakly. "And we don't know a soul in Shoal Harbour. There'll be no guests at our wedding."

"We don't need wedding guests; we've got each other," said Paddy with that warmth she couldn't resist. "Don't worry, Emmie, it's going to be fine. I've got it all arranged—the minister down there will turn a blind eye to me being Catholic."

The minister was waiting for them at the church doorway. He was bald with just a few strands of copper-red hair that were blowing hard and straight into the air. A set smile made deep creases at the corners of his eyes. With each gust of wind, his black robes flew, and their shiny purple trim caught the glint of the late-afternoon sun. He beckoned to them, seemed anxious to get on with the ceremony, as if they were keeping him from his tea.

Emily watched Paddy's easy manner as he shook the minister's hand. "Patrick Roche from Horans, and this is my gorgeous bride, Emily James from Deep Harbour."

Gorgeous bride, what a thing to say to the minister.

Now she was working hard at beating back the tears. The minister nodded in her direction, commented on the weather, then turned his back to her and gave the door a hard push with his shoulder.

Inside the church porch, the trapped air was stale with the smell of ancient wallpaper and spiders' webs. The minister cleared his throat, sending an echo through the rafters.

"The witness is not here yet. She'll be along shortly. In the meantime, Mr. Roche, we have forms to fill in."

Emily stood waiting in the porch. The hem of her blue taffeta dress was still wet from the spray on the boat ride. A shiver went through her.

My God, I never pictured my wedding day like this.

She looked inside the empty church, its old pews, worn smooth and sunken. How many young couples have taken their vows here in this church? She could sense their presence: it was hopeful, but not just that. There was something weary, too. It was a strong feeling she had that day. She often wondered about it.

Imagine having a sense of doom on your wedding day.


Years later, her daughter would beg for details about the wedding.

"Why won't you talk about it, Mom? What a romance! You and Dad, meeting like that on the train, then running away to elope, after knowing each other for just a few weeks. Sounds like you fell madly in love."

Emily would shake her head and wave her hand in the air as if to sweep the subject away.

"Don't be askin' me about that. It was a hard old day."

A stout woman holding down her crumpled little hat came rushing into the church.

"Oh, you must be the bride! How do you do! I'm Viola Mullen, from the Women's Circle. The minister asked me to stand up for you." She was a fast talker, the words tumbled out of her mouth. "I know I'm late, but I just got home this morning, myself, from the hospital in Twillingate. I got bad nerves, girl. Me husband was lost on the ice last year."

Before the ceremony began, the minister switched on the light bulb that hung on a long wire from the ceiling. It shed an oval of dim light onto the altar. Then he took his position, formally, clasping his hands before himself.

"You may approach the altar now."

Emily's eyes glistened. Patrick winked at her. "No tears now, darlin'. Nothing to cry about."

With a flourish of gallantry, he took her arm and they went down the aisle. There was no wedding march, just the shudder of the wooden beams against the wind.

As the minister droned out his "Dearly beloved…," the side door creaked open and a few curious Shoal Islanders scuffled into the back pew.

Emily peeked over her shoulder and caught the eye of one of the women, who smiled at her.

A stranger's blessing, thought Emily, but better than none at all.

It was a brief ceremony, just the murmur of vows and a faint little sob from Emily when it came her turn to say "I do."

After the pronouncement of "man and wife," came the "You may kiss the bride." Patrick took Emily in his arms and kissed her deeply. For a moment, embarrassed by the pubic display in the dank little church, she stiffened, but then he gripped her tighter and she gave in, kissing him back.

Once the marriage formalities had been completed, they were invited to the manse for fruitcake and tea, laid out on a lace table-cloth.

Patrick, jovial as ever, was bragging to the minister. "I aced law school…my prospects are good, starting with a top-notch firm in St. John's…passing the bar next year…"

The minister feigned interest, his tiny blue eyes hidden under bushy eyebrows.

Emily was in the corner with the women. Viola Mullen was still talking a mile a minute. "None of my business, I know, dear, but why did you come down here to get married? Shouldn't you be home with your own people?"

The minister's wife listened politely, but eventually managed to get her own two cents in. "We've had no summer whatsoever this year. One gale of wind after the other. Not a good time to travel this shore. Have another piece of cake, my darling, you're a beautiful bride with those blond curls, but you do look a little thin."

There was an edge to her kindness. Emily knew that her words were laced with judgment. What she was really saying was: What are you doing down here in Shoal Island United Church marrying a Catholic?

Patrick had made arrangements for the newlyweds to spend their "first night" at the home of Ted and Minnie Drover, who took in boarders. It was late by the time they finished their tea and the men had had their drink of rum. Emily and Patrick stepped out of the minister's house, into the black night and the sharp smell of balsam fir. They followed the lumpy meadow path to the Drover house, stepping around the splats of cow-do as they moved towards the yellow haze of lamplight in the window of a house up on the hill.

Patrick took Emily by the hand and quickened the pace. "Let's go right on up to bed when we get there. Don't accept any more tea or anything. I'm done with talking for this night."

The Drovers were waiting for them at the kitchen door. A few words were exchanged. Mrs. Drover was nervous, kept smoothing down the front of her apron. Mister, wearing braces and an undershirt that displayed his beer belly, gave Patrick a big smile of male complicity, looking askance at Emily before he led them upstairs to the wedding chamber.

Mrs. Drover had put her hand-crocheted spread on the bed and a Bible on the bedside table. Otherwise, the room was bare: painted wooden planks on the floor and homemade starched curtains in the window. Patrick pushed the curtains open and looked out at the night while Emily prepared for bed. Her fancy dress rustled as she took it off and placed it on the chair. She removed her stockings and camisole carefully, folded them and hid them under the dress. Shivering, she slipped on her nightie and lay between the damp sheets while Patrick, still facing out the window, took his wedding clothes off, piece by piece. He removed the pants last, and then the underwear, methodically. Emily watched the firm muscles of his naked buttocks come into view.

Then he dowsed the lamp and there was darkness and the smell of the smoking wick. He got into bed and kissed her tenderly. "You're shivering," he said. "I'll take the chill out of you." He pulled her into his into his arms.

"Mmm, Paddy, you're warm like a furnace."

"I'm warm alright," he said, lifting her nightie. "And now Missus, you're all mine."

He climbed onto her and entered. Emily felt a sharp pain. The bedsprings jiggled and squeaked, louder and louder.

"Dear God, Paddy, the Drovers will hear us!"

"They can hear us all they want. I've got hold of my lovely wife."

Emily smiled. "Oh, you're the devil, Paddy. No shame at all."

"Come on now, darlin'. Let yourself go. Come to me."

Emily moved with Paddy's rhythm.

He moaned. She felt his breath in her ear, warm sticky fluid between her legs.

Is that it? Is it all over?

He rolled off.

Emily tingled and pulsated. After a few minutes, she stirred and got up off the bed. "Oh no! Paddy, there's blood on the sheet!"

"Don't worry, darlin'. You're a married woman now. Mrs. Drover knows all about that."

And he fell into a deep sleep, the bulk of his body heavy, like a sack of potatoes on the saggy mattress.


From a house nearby came faint accordion music and a lone voice singing.

*'Deed I is in love with you*
*Up all night in the foggy dew*

My wedding song, thought Emily.

Now I'm Emily Roche. What will Mom say? Most likely nothing. She'll just raise her eyebrows and turn her head away in disgust. She could bar the door on me over this.

Mom was ever proud of her British roots, John Wesley and his wrath of God. Her whole life had been spent marching for Methodism, her eyes full of love, full of hate. And she wouldn't have things not going her way, especially when it came to Emily's marriage.

"Next year you'll be twenty-seven—you're going to end up an old-maid schoolteacher if you don't find someone soon. Having a good job is not enough. You need a husband. And beggars can't be choosers, you know. You're tall, for a woman, and men think you're hard to handle. George Stewart from the church would make a good husband. And I'm sure he'll have you."

"George Stewart is pig ignorant. I'd die of boredom with him. Let me find my own husband, Mom."

Emily laughed to herself. Paddy's a far cry from George Stewart. Catholic. Extravagant. Good to look at. Fun to talk to. Full of foolishness. There's no place for my Paddy in Mom's world.

She thought of her Aunt Jennie. She'd also married a man who didn't belong. Uncle Jack was bone lazy and fond of the drink. Jenn was always talking about her husband.

"The-one-I-got," as she called him, "is all jokes and no money." She'd make a big show of complaining about him, but you knew she was really bragging. Jenn was crazy about her Jack.

Patrick was snoring away. Emily smiled.

Well, I guess now Paddy's "the-one-I-got."

He turned over, breathing a restful sigh, and lay against Emily's back. And she let herself go, in the warm wake of his sleep.

In the morning, the little room was full of sunlight. Emily woke in her marriage bed, Paddy's stubbly chin nuzzling the nape of her neck.


They sailed out at noon on a calm sea. The houses perched on the rocks vibrated in the brightness of the day. Patrick was full of cheer as the boat pulled away from the wharf and manoeuvred through the wooded islets in the inlet. Emily tied her bandanna tight under her chin and put her face into the wind until they reached the open water and it got too cold. Then Patrick took her down to the little cabin. Cook brought them tea in a pot that said "Newfoundland Railway," and they sat on the bunk in the faint smell of diesel oil.

The boat creaked and rocked its way slowly out to sea. Patrick had gone quiet, almost sullen. In their brief courtship, Emily had never seen him like this—a first glimmer of all the Paddy she didn't know. He stared out the porthole, looking long and hard at the thin line where the blue of the sea meets the blue of the sky. Finally, he emptied his cup, put it down on the saucer, hard, and closed his eyes, grimacing, as if someone had just shot him in the stomach with an arrow.

"Now, I know I should have told you this before, but I was afraid you wouldn't go ahead with the wedding. The truth of the matter is, my love, I'm not entirely sure Mom and Dad are going to recognize a Protestant marriage. They might make us have a Catholic ceremony in the Basilica when we get to town."

He looked at her hopefully, waiting for her to say, "It doesn't matter" or "That's all right."

Emily blanched. "You said they wouldn't mind. Now you say we have to have another whole ceremony? In the Basilica? I told you, I am *never* going to bow and scrape to those priests."

The water got rough again that afternoon. The newlyweds were seasick all the way to St. John's. When they got in, shaky on their legs, they went to the post office, as planned, to make calls to the two families.

"You go first," said Emily, expecting the worst. She listened to Paddy's muffled words through the glass door of the phone booth: "…no, a Protestant wedding."

He hung up, waited a second, then turned and slowly pushed the door open. She was to remember the sheepish look on his face for the rest of her life. "They said not to be…be…bothered coming home with a Protestant for a wife."

In a slightly raised voice, a voice that Patrick would come to dread, Emily pronounced, "There's no sense calling my family either. We'll only get the same answer. We'll just have to do without them."

Patrick put his arm around her, straining to be his charming self.

"Oh, come on, Emmie. It will all blow over."

II.

THEY ARRIVED IN the back porch around 3 o'clock—Mom's tea time. Flies buzzed and banged against the window pane. Rain hammered the roof.

"It's always blowing and raining in Deep Harbour, but don't say anything to Mom about the weather," whispered Emily, nervously. "She gets insulted."

Emily stared hard at the cracks in the enamel paint on the kitchen door.

"Paddy, my stomach's in knots. Why didn't I phone ahead?

We shouldn't be turning up like this. Mom will be…"

Inside, her mother was talking. The words were muffled, but the singsong rhythm of her Deep Harbour speech came through the door. So familiar.

The porch reeked of wet sheep's wool from the sweaters hanging on the wall hooks. Patrick shuffled his feet. "For God's sake, go on in. I'm soaked and it stinks in here."

She scrutinized him for a moment, as if to see him through her mother's eyes. Then, resolved, she grabbed the ivory knob and pushed open the door, catching Mom in mid-sentence:

"…and I told her it was simply no use asking."

As usual, Mom was tidy and composed, except for the pinkness in her cheeks that prickled red when she saw Emily in the door frame. Her hands were covered in flour, and she held her rolling pin confidently, expertly. Pastry was her great talent: no woman in the Harbour could touch her on that one.

She clapped her hands, sending a cloud of flour before herself. "We got your note about the wedding. I thought you'd turn up to see us one day. Your father wanted to write you, but—Ches, put the kettle on while I clear this table." Then she glanced at Patrick, who stood in limbo in the back porch. "Better come in and close that door before all the heat gets drawn out."

He stepped in, a hulking figure in the low-ceilinged room. Mom's hands stayed busy picking up pastry ends on the table, but her eyes rested deeply on him for a few seconds, taking him in good from head to toe. When she turned away, her face bore the look of someone who'd just had her worst fear confirmed.

Emily sat at the table, hands folded in her lap like a guest, while Mom set out the cups and saucers. That first awful moment, the sight of her mother's face, was over with. They had made it inside, into Mom's kitchen, with the spotless wiped-down counter, salt fish in soak, pie sitting ready to be baked.

Her father asked soft questions, sticking to safe topics.

"How was the road? Have they fixed that stretch near Heart's Content?" No mention whatsoever of the wedding or anything to do with their married life. "Did you see the damage to the wharf?"

He was friendly but careful, glancing over at his wife's silent presence and then falling into silence himself when she put the hot teapot on the oilcloth, wiped her hands in her apron, and sat down.

She talked, but there was a drag in her voice, like you hear at funerals. "Uncle Ron's in Boston and Maude's goin' up next month."

It was all news of this aunt or that uncle, the tight mesh of people that Emily had walked away from. But she could still feel the gravity of it all pulling her—the roundness of her mother's belly under the flowered apron, her plain hands; her father, smiling in his benign way. He was always in the same posture, arms clutching the sides of the rocker, only ever half listening, somewhere out on the edge of it all.

Mom put a few buns out on a plate and poured the tea. She hadn't bothered with the good cups. It was just the old kitchen set with the "Jolly Sleigh Ride" pattern that Emily had so loved as a child—horses prancing in a snowy field, pulling a sleigh full of happy children with bright eyes, rosy cheeks, scarves flying. Over and over, she had dreamed she was riding along in that sleigh, having the time of her life.

There was a lull in the talk. This was Emily's chance. She looked straight at her mother, then turned her body slightly towards Patrick and said, tenuously, "Patrick's got an articling position with a law firm in town. We've rented a flat, on Plank Road, just up from the railway station."

"Your Aunt Kit's first husband grew up on that street. I remember him saying it was rough," said Mom, with disgusted emphasis on *rough*.

Patrick snuck a wry smile at Emily, as if to say, "So this is the dreaded disapproval." Emily squirmed and crossed her legs. The one thing she didn't want was for Mom to get in her critical mode. That rock-hard refusal. Mom's veto. It still hit her hard in the gut. And, of course, now Paddy decides to get all full of his own charm.

"True enough. Plank Road's gone down a bit, but me and Emily are bringin' up the tone." He laughed, putting his hand on Emily's knee.

A thought crossed her mind.

I bet he had a drink on the sly before we got the taxi.

"Sure, Emmie keeps our place done up like the Taj Mahal—"

Mom cut in like a knife. "What's this *Emmie*? No one here calls her that. She's Emily to us."

Patrick grinned, gloriously handsome.

Not to be outdone, Mom grinned back. "Those little-girl names just don't suit Emily's nature." And then, with mirth in her eye, she added. "But you haven't known her all that long."

Emily had seen her mother do that before—turn on a dime, from sour to playful. Mom enjoyed a little banter with a man. Emily remembered her flirty chats with Mr. Connery, the butcher who brought fresh meat to the door. A big strapping man with lively brown eyes, he'd carry on with Mom in the doorway, squeezing her arm in the delicious part of the joke. Little Emily would be embarrassed. Why didn't Mom ever joke like that with Dad? Poor Dad was relegated to a single role—stay quiet and pay homage. He still carried an old sepia photo of Mom in his wallet—a pretty young thing in a flapper dress and white stockings, posing at a summer picnic.

A thundering shower pelted hard against the window pane. They all turned and looked out at the sight of it. Through the sheets of rain you could see the water in the harbour, churning. For a moment, against the black turbulence of the outdoors, the yellow light and warmth of the kitchen brought the four of them together.

But Mom wasn't having any such thing. "Best clear these dishes, now," she said, jumping to her feet. Her unbaked pie was still sitting on the counter. The oven was good and ready but she'd made no move to put it in. The kitchen was getting close; steam was forming on the windows. Mom stood at the sink with her back to them, rattling the dishes in the soapy water. Emily looked over at Patrick and made a motion with her eyes that they should leave. But just as they were rising from their chairs, the door flew open and in stepped Dad's younger sister, Aunt Jennie.

"Let me in for God's sake! I'm soaked to the bone."

Good old Aunt Jenn. More than once, she'd appeared, like an angel, when Emily needed her.

"Well, look who's here! My favourite niece!" Wet coat and all, she threw her arms around Emily. Then she turned to Patrick. "Don't mind me. I'm always turning up at the wrong time, like a bad penny."

Mom didn't turn around. She didn't approve of Jennie, her vulgar clothes, her lack of shame about her drinking husband. "There's no need for Jennie to be gettin' on with the like of that," Mom would preach. "You can't help your failings, but faults *can be corrected*."

Jenn ploughed ahead. "How long are you staying for? You'll have to come over and have a drop of rum with Jack."

Patrick beamed. "Now that's an offer I can't refuse. I'm always—" but he stopped in mid-sentence, realizing, for once, how deeply out of turn he was.

The air went dead.

There was a big splash in the kitchen sink. Mom lifted her hands out of the dishwater and, still with her back to the room, pronounced, "They'll be staying for a few nights—at least until the flower service at the cemetery on Sunday."

Emily and Patrick were quick to take their cue and settle directly back into their chairs. Dad went to move their damp coats out of the porch and into the hall closet. And Mom put her pie in the oven.

Aunt Jennie started right in on all the unspeakable topics. "How was the wedding? Too bad we didn't get to celebrate! And what are your plans now? Startin' a big family? S'pose you will, bein' Catholic and all."

Emily couldn't take her eyes off Mom. Finally, she got up to dry the dishes. Mom passed her an apron, hand embroidered with little violets. "That was your Nan's," she said, "I was going to give it to you."

Emily felt a ripple of relief.

The rain stopped at suppertime. The clouds shunted off and the setting sun put on a show out the kitchen window. There was talk over supper but it was strained and eventually went stagnant. It was Dad, surprisingly, who decided to stir things up.

"Now, tell me Patrick," he said, defying Mom's stare. "You must have a big job on your hands at the courts."

Patrick squared his shoulders and slipped into his lawyer pose: confident, fluid. "Lawyers are a corrupt nation," he said, taking a quick look to see if he had Mom's attention. "You'd be surprised by what goes on in the halls of justice."

Mom remained blank-faced, but Emily knew she was listening carefully, sorting and filtering, as usual.

Patrick regaled Dad with his struggles to withstand the forces of evil. "I need to get ahead," he concluded, earnestly. "But I'll have no truck with their tricks and lies."

A crack appeared in Mom's facade. "It can be hard to keep on the straight and narrow," she said, with all the weight of her wisdom. "That takes moral fibre."

*Moral fibre*, thought Emily. Paddy'd better shut up now while he's ahead.

After supper, time came for dessert—Mom's blueberry pie, warm and juicy with pastry pinched into perfect scallops around the edge of the dish. She placed it on a stand in the middle of the table.

"Now, I hope this is all right," she said, with false modesty. "The berries were small and scarce this year."

"No one in my family could ever make a pie like that," said Patrick.

Mom gave him a crooked half-smile.

Encouraged, he continued. "My mother's no pastry chef but a fine woman for all that…" And off he went. "Three boys to rear…grand old house…my father being a judge, has to be away from home…respected all over…"

Mom served him another cut of pie. "I'm sure your father has to deal with the worst kind of rabble." She passed him the clotted cream. "I admire those judges."

Patrick served himself a generous dollop of cream. "Oh, Dad's the finest kind. Emily's met my Mom and Dad, you know. We had a lovely visit. It went really well, didn't it, darlin'?"

Emily shuddered. If only Mom knew the truth.


Emily throws the sheets off.

"You know, Paddy, you shouldn't be lying like that. Telling Mom I met your parents. Making yourself out to be a saint."

Patrick mumbles from his half-sleep. "But it worked out good—she's all impressed now."

"You really have a way of stretching the truth. It's going catch up with you one of these days."

Paddy opens his eyes. "Well, you're going to meet Mom and Dad, eventually. And you got what you wanted, didn't you? We're here sleeping under your parents' roof. So stop your moralizing. I'm fed up to the teeth with it."

He pulls the sheet tight over his shoulder.

Emily hears Mom's step on the stairs, slow and steady. A few seconds later, a faint "Good night, now," comes through the door. Then her footsteps continue up the stairs to her room on the next landing.

Mom went against herself today, let down her guard. Maybe it's not such a bad thing Patrick pulled her into his net.

Dad comes up a little while later, tiptoeing so as not to disturb anyone. Emily hears him open Mom's door and murmur a few low words. Then the door clicks shut, and he goes to his own room directly across. Emily smiles to herself. She knows their ritual, their funny way of loving. In the daytime, Mom is curt and cross with Dad, but at bedtime she always speaks nicely to him, smoothing everything over before they head separately into the night.

Emily slips out of bed and opens the window a crack, feeling the nip of salt air. She looks out at the stars perched on the tips of the black hills. Why did this view always make her sad? Why did the beauty of it always feel so out of reach? Like the jolly sleigh ride she never got to go on.

She gets back under the covers. Patrick's warm body fills the empty side of the bed, the part that had always remained smooth and cool.

He's lived through the day unconcerned, she thinks, and I'm still here in the wars.

She snuggles in.

III.

THE TALK WAS all property.

"Eugene Garland let that place run down a long time ago." Patrick put his arms around his two brothers' shoulders. "But we're goin' to make something of that land."

There was clinking of glasses and rumble of male voices.

Emily called into the parlour from the doorway, "Paddy, let's go on upstairs, now." But she couldn't even catch his eye.

Emily and Patrick had arrived at the Roche house in the dark of night by bay taxi. She couldn't see much of Horans, but it seemed like a prosperous town, with its fishing premises, large church and attached convent.

They rose late the next morning. Paddy's mother was waiting in the dining room, where just the three of them ate the warmed-over breakfast. Mrs. Roche turned the side of her face to Emily and talked straight at Patrick. It was strange talk to Emily—long, breathy sentences that seemed to weasel and swoop around the middle of what was being said.

"Of course, there's no need to let old Eugene know anything

just now…Your father's found a way to arrange things."

Eventually, Missus stood up with a cup of tea in her hand and turned to Emily.

"Come along to the front room now, my dear," she summoned, "for a little chat."

Emily had imagined her mother-in-law as a warm-bosomed matriarch, a sort of Queen Mother. Now she had to confront the flesh and blood of the real Meaghan Roche. Emily followed her down the long corridor to the other end of the house, taking a good look at her from the back. Her head was small and well groomed but her hips flared out, making her dress hang like curtains from the sides. She was talking over her shoulder, bobbing her head as if she was really trying to get a point across. Still chatting away as she entered the front room, she directed Emily to the couch and sat down herself in the large chair opposite, filling its breadth completely.

In the dusty slats of sunshine that streamed in though French doors, the two women made question-and-answer talk.

"Now, my dear," said Mrs. R., her gray eyes cold as glacier pebbles, "tell me about your people."

"Well, my mother does some part-time teaching and my father has his own boat. And I myself am a school teacher. I'm applying for a position in town. I hope to—"

"You won't need to be doin' that anymore now you've got Patrick," she said, turning her head to the window as if there were something of much greater import out in the garden.

Emily glanced around the room. Before she married Patrick, she'd never been past the front gate of a place like this. The house was a showpiece, with kept grounds and wraparound verandas. But it wasn't really all that grand once you got inside. There was a silver candelabra and velvet curtains, like you'd expect in the home of a judge, but everything was tarnished and faded. On the mantle was an expensive-looking porcelain figurine, a dancing nobleman, in court attire. But he was cracked and chipped, with gobs of glue joining his arms to his shoulders. Next to that was a framed picture of the Roches in their finery, standing with the

Archbishop on the steps of his Palace. Missus wore a black lacy veil over her head, like Jackie Kennedy visiting the Pope.

"Emily my *daarlin*, don't be looking too close at that dusty old mantle."

Emily blurted, "I'd be happy to help out with the cleaning." But she knew immediately she'd said the wrong thing.

Missus pulled her sweater around her belly and said pointedly, with knit eyebrows, "Oh, no, no my dear. There's no need for you to do any of that. The *girl* will do it on Monday."

That night, at the dinner table, the old judge reigned supreme, pumping out stories and jokes with a slick, radio announcer voice.

No trouble to see where Paddy got the charm, thought Emily. And Paddy's two brothers, Sean and Shamus, had it too— the swarthy good looks, the gift of the gab.

All topics of conversation were set by the judge and cut off when he wished to change the subject. His wife and children were adept at moving from topic to topic without missing a beat.

"Eugene Garland is an uneducated bumpkin," said the judge, shaking his jowls. "He wouldn't know a contract from a hole in the wall!" A flash of loathing crossed his face. "People like that shouldn't be sittin' on valuable land."

"The Roches are on the march again," said Shamus.

"This time we're goin' to hit gold," said Patrick. "Property development. No stoppin' us now."

Is that the whiskey talking? Emily wondered. He seems like he's play-acting.

All day, Paddy had been strutting around the house with his chest puffed out, talking a blue streak. "I couldn't be happier, Emmie. God bless that priest for tyin' us up. Now you're part of the family. Did you ever see such a card as Dad? And, of course, Mom's a saint for puttin' up with us all."

To top it all off, Emily had overheard him telling his brothers that she and her mother-in-law had developed "a real bond."

Some bond that is, thought Emily. There's only one bond

in this house—between the Roches. When Mrs. says, "Emily, my love, don't worry about that," she really means, "Stay away from that."

Emily had never met anyone like her mother-in-law. Here was a woman who could bank on empty afternoons for the rest of her life—nothing to do but sit around, all powdered up, with her earrings on, just to listen to the radio.

"You're going to be the daughter Mom never had," Patrick had said, his eyes tearing up.

Emily could only think of the hard-earned, bedrock bond she had with her own mother, who'd never had an idle day in her life.

What have I got into, with these Roches? she wondered. I'll never fit in here. And to think I went through the trouble to get married in their church just to please them, keep Paddy in the fold.


As Patrick had warned, the Roches had refused to recognize his Protestant marriage to Emily.

Paddy had reacted offhandedly to the veto. "It's just a matter of getting a Catholic marriage certificate. Don't worry, Em, it won't mean anything. It's just to please Mom and Dad."

"This goes against my grain. I told you I don't want to bow and scrape to those priests," she'd said gravely. "But there's no other way out. You can't lose touch with your family. We'll have to get the Catholic certificate."

The wedding vows in the Basilica in St. John's were simply a formality. On a sunny October morning, Patrick and Emily signed papers in a chilly little office in the back of the church. All her life, Emily would tell the story of that day, how she "looked the priest right in the eye and told a big lie: 'I vow I will raise my children in the Catholic faith.'"

Another story Emily often told was about what happened after they'd left the priest's office that morning. Marriage certificate in hand, they'd slipped out the side door of the church.

As they turned the corner of the building, they ran into a big wedding party that had just come down the steps of the main entrance. The party was all in full regalia, the groom and attendants in tuxedos, the bride in a massive lace gown and her cohort of bridesmaids in stiff red dresses.

"I know who the bride is," said Paddy. "She's the Archbishop's niece. Look at all the priests and nuns milling around in the crowd."

"Quick, let's get out of here," said Emily, "I feel like a complete hypocrite."

The next morning, while the Roches were sleeping it off, Emily was pounding along the path across the field to the Garland property. She buttoned her coat against the morning fog. This is none of my business, and Paddy'd be mad if he knew what I was up to, but mad he'll have to be. I want to see this place for myself.

Away from the house, the ground got spongy and wet, squelching under her feet, but she kept going until she reached the edge of the Roche property, where it touched on the old Garland plantation. Then there was a short climb up a steep hill and a long look down at the back of the Garland cottage.

The house below looked forlorn, like no one had given it any attention for a long time. In the windows, there were yellowing lace curtains, disintegrating on their very rods. And the whole structure tilted to one side, as if it were slowly melting into the ground. She moved down the hill, stepping around the rocks and gullies. At the back of the house, she found a group of old gravestones. Some stood at precarious angles, while others lay flat, like smooth steps. Their grainy engravings, blackened and eaten by lichen, were barely visible, but Emily got down on her knees and deciphered the Garland name on them—generations had been born and died on this very spot.

"Excuse me, Missus. Is you looking for someone?" The old man stood leaning on his cane. "I was just goin' out to the shed and saw you come down the hill."

Emily scrambled to her feet. This is the very thing the Roches didn't want. Last night, the judge had laid down the law: "No more contact with Garland till we pull this off."

"How do you do, Mr. Garland. My name is Emily Roche. Just came over to say hello. I'm Patrick's wife."

"He's a fine fellow, your husband. He was just over here yesterday. Helpin' me out with this old place. Being a lawyer and all, he knows how to handle land deeds. He'll see me right, for sure."

He motioned, cupping his hand. "Come on 'round to the front and see my cabbage patch, my pride and joy."

She followed him as he turned the corner of the house, loping and swaying, his hips stiff in their hinges.

"Look at this here," he said, pointing with his cane.

It was a big patch—all set out in neat rows—dark leaves unfurling around waxy cabbage heads, lined up in the fog like green cannonballs.

"These will be the last ones I'll ever take out of this ground." He looked away, then turned back. "But it's time for me to give it up, see."


"Sure that crowd of Garlands never did a day's work in their lives," said Mrs. Roche. Her unflicked cigarette ash dropped off and rolled down the front of her dress. "They fair lived on dole rations."

Emily sat in silence, watching her mother-in-law holding forth from her throne. She's speaking in an exaggerated, lilting way tonight, her eyes full of complicity with her handsome sons.

"And in the old days, they had babies like rabbits in that little saltbox."

Emily pictured the old plantation and the cabbages. I'm just a speck of dust in here. They have no idea of who I am, what I think.

They knew nothing of the patch she grew in, a house where actions are judged, pennies pinched, words measured, and not a drop of liquor crosses the doorstep. The worst thing was, not even Paddy seemed to know. He'd been chatting away at her glum silences, unfazed.

"Garland's two sons are long gone out of here. They went off to the States during the Depression," said Shamus, pouring himself a fresh drink. "They've been out of touch for years. Old Eugene would have to give the land to the Church anyway, wouldn't he?"

"And would the Methodists know what to do with it?" said Patrick, laughing as he took Emily's hand.

At the touch of his fingers, she stood up and announced to the room: "I'm off to bed. Best I leave that property talk to you people. Since I don't come from that world."

As she closed the door, she saw the Roches exchange mocking grimaces, raising their eyebrows and pursing their lips.


She sat on the edge of the bed, fully dressed.

Is this the real Paddy? Can we ever go back to the way we were?

Life had been fun and full of high jinks in the honeymoon apartment. On Saturday nights they danced to the radio in the kitchen and on Sunday mornings, they stayed in bed, cooing and love-making. There were even plans to have a baby, sooner than later.

Emily heard footsteps outside the door. Patrick came in, glowing red in the cheeks. He stretched out on the covers, hands clasped behind his head, chipper.

"Mom sent me up to see if you're okay. What are you sulking about? We're having a grand visit, aren't we?"

"How can you go along with all this, Paddy?"

"With what?"

"That old man trusts you. He thinks you're giving him a good price."

"Of course he trusts us, the Roches are a highly respected

family. He'll take whatever we offer him, and consider himself damn lucky."

There was something nasty nibbling around the edge of his words.

"No son of Garland's is ever going to turn up. Our family's going to make a massive contribution to land development in this region. This project is another example—"

Emily sliced in. "You can convince yourself of your own lies, but the fact of the matter is, you Roches are stealing that land."

Patrick averted his eyes. But almost immediately, he recovered and put on a smirky smile. "Now don't be going back to your fire and brimstone, my little Protestant maid." He pinched her nipple between his thumb and forefinger. "We're not running a charity society here. You've got to learn how property deals work."

He put his arm around her shoulder. "Don't go turnin' sour on me now, Emmie. Never mind all that." He pulled her in. "Come here and give me a kiss."

She sprang away, banging her elbow against the wall.

In a flash, his face changed to the same hateful expression she'd seen on his father's face. He jumped off the bed and stood over her. "My brothers were right. You're a real miss uppity, too righteous to have a drink with the rest of us. Just who do you think you are?"

He headed for the door, swaggering, but changed his mind and got back on the bed. He lay down, turning his face to the wall.

"Sorry Emmie, I shouldn't be yelling at you like that," he mumbled, as he fell asleep. "But what would a fisherman's daughter like you know about property?"

"Fishermen know the difference between cheating and honesty," said Emily. "You can't just roll over me like that."

But Patrick was already snoring, leaving Emily to the night noises, taps running and doors shutting as the Roches went to bed. Emily lay back on the pillow, next to her handsome husband. Was he still the Paddy she'd married?

Downstairs, sticky liquor glasses and full ashtrays sat

waiting to be picked up off arms of chairs.

### IV.

EMILY STIRRED HER tea and placed the hot spoon on the saucer.

"I was hoping that now we're back in town, you'd forget about that property nonsense. We can't afford to invest in a housing development, Paddy. And we're not going to start borrowing money. I won't go down that road."

"I know you'd rather starve than owe a cent to anyone, Emmie. But how else are we goin' to get the funds to buy you a nice little house? It'll take me years to build up a law practice. And, anyway, I'm not one for scrimpin' and savin'."

"You can say that again. I'm home mending my stockings while you're out riding around in taxis like a millionaire. Too bad I didn't get that teaching position, we're going to need an extra check coming in."

Patrick flashed his big smile. "I'll get ya new stockings, darlin'. All the stockings in the world. And don't you worry about getting a job. We'll be fine when this deal comes through. We just need to put some money towards it."

He reached across the table and took her hand. "Come on now. Let's turn the radio on and have a little dance."

He set the dial to the VOWR Saturday Night Dance Party. The jazzy saxophone riffs of "In the Mood" filled the apartment.

"All right, in the name of God," said Emily, standing up. She couldn't resist a dance with her Paddy.

He swung her around the kitchen. "We do have our good times, don't we, Emmie James?"

It was true: Emily had had her good times with Paddy. But, for the past few months, she'd been finding it harder to get off her chair and dance. With Paddy running off to connive in land development with the Roches and all the uncertainty about money, the worry was creeping into her, seizing her. And to add to her misery, she was having to endure regular visits from her mother-in-law. "Parked in the living room like Queen Tut waiting to be served a drink," as Emily put it.

Emily was determined to keep the drinking modest. She had a set of coloured sherry glasses, mostly stem, with a tiny cup, big enough for two sips of liquor. She'd bring them out on a tray with great ceremony—yellow ones, blue ones, red ones, all rattling on their skinny stems. Mrs. Roche would down her drink in one fell swoop. That was a drop in the bucket for her. But it didn't matter because she always had a flask of whiskey in her big tapestry bag. She'd go to the bathroom and have a swig and douse herself in perfume, but you could still smell the booze off her when she came out.

In her cups, she'd lord it over Emily, advising her on what was wrong with the apartment, her love nest with Paddy that she had so carefully decorated. The advice consisted mostly of fault finding with Emily's taste: the cushions were "cheap looking" or "didn't match the couch, "the lamps were "too dim."

Once she'd finished with her critiques, she she'd drawl on about the glory of the Roches and their plans. "Now that we finally got our hands on Eugene Garland's plantation, we can go ahead and start our project—just think, a brand new subdivision with fifteen houses. And that's only the beginning. There's a lot of money at stake."

Money we don't have, thought Emily. Pie in the sky.


"I'm calling from the collection agency, about your unpaid light and power bills," said the nasal voice on the phone. "And there are also the telephone bills."

Collection agency? Emily had to pull up a chair and sit down before she could respond. "There must be some mistake," she said, gulping.

"Oh no, there's no mistake, Mrs. Roche. You are three months in arrears with both utilities."

Emily had barely hung up and was sitting in the chair, shaken, when the phone rang again. This time it was Paddy's law office calling to leave a message that her husband should "come in to sign the severance papers."

Severance papers?

When Patrick came in late that night, Emily was waiting for him pale and tense.

He sat on the couch in his overcoat. Emily stood over him, hands on her hips, chiding him like a child.

As angry as she was and as much as she lectured him about giving up a perfectly good job and putting her in the shame of debt, Paddy remained buoyant and calm.

He crossed his legs in his devil-may-care way. Then he laid it all out for her. It was plain and simple. There was no need to worry—being out of the law firm and in the land business full time, he'd bring in floods of money, more than enough to pay the bills and buy her "a real swank of a house."

He lit a cigarette. A picture of confidence. "You'll see, Em."

Emily flew at him. "I'll see nothing. You're trying to act like a tycoon, going around with a big briefcase and a fancy suit. But it's all false. It's that mother of yours and her high notions."

Emily knew she'd hit Patrick's tender spot—criticizing his mother was taboo. Red in the face, he stood up.

"That's not fair, Em. You know very well that Mom has the best business head of any of us."

This time, Emily went for broke. "Your mother's a fake. She's got no head for business. That woman just wants her precious boys to make the big time—a housing development no less. She'll drive you all into the ground."

The pitch of Patrick's voice went high. "Mom's the finest kind, Emmie," he squealed. "And you know she thinks the world of you."


In the dead of a winter's night, ice cracked on the bedroom window. Emily lay awake. It ends up I'm married to Paddy *and* his mother. Three in the marriage bed, as they say. Can I ever push her out? Get Paddy away from her scheming? He and I could make a go of it if only he'd finish his articling, pass the bar.

Her mind kept churning until, eventually, she got up, put on her slippers and crept into the kitchen to make tea. When she turned on the light, a mouse scurried under the stove.

Something else I can't control, she thought. It's this drafty old building with its cracks and holes. Mice coming and going as they please.

As she filled the kettle, she noticed that Paddy had left his briefcase sitting out on the counter. That's the one thing he was usually careful about, putting the case away in the closet, out of her sight. She put the kettle down.

I have a right to know where all this financing is coming from.

Her fingers fiddled with the brass clasp. It was cold and stiff but she got it open. Her hand dove in and shuffled through the papers. The one that caught her eye had the red letterhead of the Bank of Nova Scotia and the address of the Water Street branch where she and Paddy had their joint account. She slipped it out.

What she saw under *Withdrawals* changed everything. She stood frozen with the paper in her hand.

Paddy appeared in the doorway in his pyjamas. "I can explain, Emmie."

Emily threw the paper at him. It fluttered to his feet. "How low can you go, Paddy," she hissed. "That was a wedding gift from Mom and Dad. The few savings they'd made by dint of their own hard work. God knows, they don't know anything about having debts or taking other people's money. They called the other day to see how we're doing, and I had to lie—I could never let on to them about our unpaid bills and the mess we're in. And now you've up and stolen the nest egg they gave us!"

"We were struggling with financing for the next phase of the development—Sean and Shamus ran into bad luck, lost their shirts on that other project…"

A spray of ice pellets hit the kitchen window. Emily shivered, put her arms around herself. "You promised me you'd never touch those savings."

"But we're going to get that money back in spades…"

"Those developers are nothing but a bunch of crooks. And you Roches are too pumped up with ambition to know better."

"Come on, Em. You'll be happy enough to be a Roche when the money starts rolling in."

"Don't include me in your skulduggery," she shouted. "I'm a Roche by name only. And I thank God for that."

She turned her back. There was a moment's silence before she spoke. This time her voice was almost a whisper.

"Now get out of my sight. I can't stand to look at you."


*Can't stand to look at you.* Emily had imposed her veto, as severe a judgement as her own mother had ever made. She knew that Paddy couldn't bear to be shut out by her—usually, she found a way to forgive him for his recklessness, hoping he would mend his ways. But this time, she declared Cold War. The apartment on Plank Road, the little love nest that had been filled with music and chatter, went quiet. She stayed in the spare room with the door closed, cursing herself for ever thinking she'd get to own a home in the Housing.

*Dreaming of dollhouses, like a youngster. How foolish was I.*

Guilty and cowed, Patrick tried everything to get back into her good books. He kept the kitchen clean and washed the dirty dishes, rinsing them carefully the way Emily liked and putting them away in the cupboard as silently as he could: an act of contriteness, to show her that he knew just how bad he had been. But there was no cajoling her this time.

Alone in the spartan spare room with a single bed and no rug on the floor, she listened to the mice scratching while she battled with her own absolutes. What Paddy had done went against her very fibre, but, for all that, she was finding it hard to stay up on her high horse. She thought of her mother's stern surmisal of marriage, how it often came down to a wife to reform her husband and "make a man of him."

Should I give Paddy a chance? Am I being too harsh on him? If I forgive him, I'm as bad as he is…but I can't be barred in here forever…

After a month of purgatory, Paddy was getting desperate. One evening when the March wind was howling outside, he knocked on her door. But she refused to answer. He called out to her in his boyish, dependant way, "Please, Emmie, come sit and listen to the news with me. It's a shockin' old night. I'm all alone out here." But she still didn't answer, afraid he would notice that she was aching for him, longing for the oneness with him that had vanquished the old lonely self she didn't want to go back to.

Later, she heard him pacing the floors. Happy-go-lucky Paddy, who usually snored his way through the night, no matter what the crisis, was finding no rest.

Then one day, Paddy's mother came knocking at the door. Paddy brought her into the living room, but Emily didn't go out to greet her. She listened to them talking, first murmuring, then raising their voices.

"But I've got to pull out of the business, Mom. This is ruining my marriage."

"What kind of marriage is that? When you can't be a man, make money to get ahead? Your father will be disgusted with you for being so soft. And how can you let down your brothers like that? Sean and Shamus will gutted when they hear about this."

She's going to have her way again, thought Emily. Paddy can't withstand her.

But to Emily's surprise, this time, Paddy stood his ground.

"It's hopeless trying to stop me, Mom. I want my wife back. I've made up my mind. I'm pulling out."

Emily could hear the clinking of Meaghan Roche's car keys as she took them out of her purse.

"Don't go stomping out in huff, Mom," said Paddy in his high voice. "We'll work out some arrangement for the money."

Too UNSPEAKABLE for Words

"I never thought a son of mine would betray me, but if you're that weak, we're better off without you," retaliated the old matriarch. "So go ahead, let that wife of yours lead you around by the nose, if that's what you want."

Before long, Patrick was back working at the law firm. When bank statements came in the mail, he left them on the counter so Emily could see that his wages were going straight into their account.

April came and spring light filled the sad little apartment, drawing Emily out from behind her closed doors. On Easter Sunday morning, with the church bells ringing on Patrick Street and the Halleluyah Chorus booming from the kitchen radio, she came to the breakfast table. Then, as time passed, with the bills slowly being paid off and no threat that Meaghan Roche would turn up unannounced in a fox fur wrap with liquor on her breath and land deeds in her hand, Emily allowed herself to warm up. In some painful way, she was winning back her marriage, imperfect as it was.

"Now will you forgive me?" said Paddy one night, when he'd finally managed to get her laughing over the supper table. "I know I was a devil—it was ugly what I did. I have a lot to account for. But I promise you, Emily Roche, I may not be an angel, but I'm chastened, a changed man. And it's for good."

Patrick looked into Emily's face. Only a faint hint remained of the hurt that had contorted her features all these months. Her natural prettiness was shining through. He touched her hair. "My soft blond wife with the steel principles. I never want to lose you. Now let's turn on the radio and have a dance." He took her hand and she let him pull her up from the chair.

She put her arm around Paddy's shoulders.

"I'm not sure we'll ever dance to the same tune," she said, with a crack of a smile.

# LA FACHADA

FACED WITH THE prospect of a long "Holy Week" of solitude, I booked a ticket to Santiago de Cuba, where the Revolution had wiped Easter off the calendar many years before.

After a sleepless night at the beach hotel, I asked the tour guide to find me a quiet room in town, away from the party-seekers. I ended up in a private house—a *casa particular* or *kaasah paartikulaaar* as I said with my accent, when I turned up at their door.

"Yes, this is the *kaasah*, do come in," said Gabí, the owner, teasing me with irresistible affection, as if we were already friends. I was immediately drawn to his lively attention.

Gabí and his wife, Rosa, proudly showed me through the house, a crumbling villa on a hill in the old quarter. The rooms were arranged around a shaded patio in the back. It had a spectacular view. We stood looking out over the city as it tumbled away from the terrace. Rosa pointed to a white tower. "That's the college where Fidel studied," she said, pronouncing the word "Fidel" with intimacy, as if he were a family member. Behind me, someone stepped onto the patio.

"*Buenas tardes*," said a silky female voice that made my head turn.

My first sight of Milagros—ravishing in a blue dress against her dark skin.

"Please, meet our daughter," said Rosa. "She teaches violin at the Music School. Milagros, this is our guest, Max. He's a teacher too."

I reached my hand out but she leaned right in and kissed me on the cheek. As I stood, dazed, an adolescent girl in a school uniform appeared in the doorway holding a flute.

"And this is our granddaughter, Vivian."

The girl was as radiant and composed as her mother. "Nice to meet you," she said, giving me my second kiss on the cheek.

"You must join us for a drink on the patio later," said Gabí. "Full moon tonight."

Out under the moon, the conversation was animated, delicious. Gabí, chain-smoking and quick-minded, kept the ideas flowing. He looked up at the sky. "In Santería, the new moon means a chance to refresh your senses."

Knowing precious little about Santería, I struggled to catch the tone of Gabí's comment. Was it light or heavy, funny or philosophical?

"Refresh your senses," I repeated stiffly, "Sounds like a wonderful opportunity." And as for my senses, they were already on overload. The soft air was falling on my white arms, caressing me. A breeze rustled through the palms, wafting in the sound of bongos, congas and other drums.

Milagros sat next to me with her lovely bare shoulders, round and smooth. "Those are ritual drummers, preparing for the *rumba* at the end of the week" she said, intriguingly.

"The *rumba*," I said. "Is that some kind of Santería ceremony?"

"Very much so," she said, "That's when you *really* get refreshed. We'll invite you along."

After my second rum, I heard myself holding forth: "They

say my family has Spanish blood through the sailors stranded on the Irish coast from the shipwrecked Spanish Armada, and, of course, there are old historical Newfoundland–Cuba trade routes. We've been dealing with each other for hundreds of years."

Oh yes. For once in my life I was flirting, emitting as much charm as I could muster. Out of the corner of my eye, I could see that my hosts were perplexed by the idea of me being Spanish. But they egged me on.

"Trade with Terra Nova…very interesting."

"*Muy interesante*," I ventured, in my internet Spanish.

Milagros beamed at me. "Very good! If you want, I'll help you practice speaking."


The next afternoon, Milagros and I sat together at the table on the terrace for a Spanish lesson. Such a lesson. She was luscious, so luscious that I had to close my eyes, or look away, to stop myself from gaping.

She looked African, and I noticed a delicate touch of Chinese around her eyes—clear, amber, playful eyes that turned a language lesson into a teasingly fascinating event.

"*Me calles bien*," she said, "I like you!"

Her Spanish rolled over her lips, warm and sensual, like the turquoise waves that roll into Santiago Bay. No hint of the guttural Iberian sounds I'd repeated so slavishly on the internet.

"*Ahora tú*…Now you tell me…"

I pursed my dry lips around the delectable words. She laughed at me, laying her hand on my knuckles, enticing me out of my chaste self. I sat there in the sticky heat, breathless from being so close to her.

"Tell me about yourself. I know you have a good heart," she said, patting my chest with her pink fingertips.

"Oh, I used to be in the Holy Orders, spent lots of time learning to be good," I answered as suavely as I could.

In my mind, I was already cursing myself. Why did I have to reveal the priest thing so early in the game?

"And what was it that lured you out of the priesthood?"

I rallied. "Well, it's a long story," I said, fixing my eyes on her. "But let's just say I was not cut out for celibacy."

What a show I was putting on! Max-the-Latin-Lover, so nervous that my few strands of hair were drenched and sticking like glue to my bald scalp.

That night, I tossed and turned on the lumpy mattress in my hot little room. For all the flirtation on the terrace, I was spending the night alone on the sticky sheets, pulsating and pondering. Am I just another old fool? Coming down here, falling in love? I've heard of Cubans charming the pants off foreigners, getting married to "trampoline" themselves off the island. I thought of my old Aunt Win's warning: "You'd better be careful with women. You're too good-hearted. They'll walk all over you."

All those years in the Orders I'd tried to dowse my fires of lust, not that they'd ever been that ardent. I barely had the collar off my neck when my bossy Aunt Win got busy matchmaking. "There's no time to waste, now, Max. Newly de-frocked priests need to go right out on the prowl."

But let's face it, I was no Don Juan.

"I know what you get on with," said Aunt Win. "All that priest talk will never seduce any woman."

After a string of courting disasters, she resigned herself to the fact that I was "bookish" and "flabby" and "still clinging to the vows."

Now, here in this Cuban night, there were flickers in me and they were flaring.

The Spanish lessons on the patio continued. Milagros and I were speeding along. Or so I thought. Within a day, we'd developed our own language, our own discourse, on all manner of topics—the first world, the third world, *socialismo*, religion. Rosa and Gabí seemed pleased by our discussions. They'd smile at us from the kitchen door, or serve us coffee and little tropical fruits, as if to encourage us.

"The Church has its good points," I bantered one afternoon when Milagros had been criticizing organized religion. "Think of the liberation fathers in Central America," I said, savouring the pervasive sexuality in the air, in the very syntax.

"The Cuban Catholic Church," she said, stirring the pot to keep a nice edge on the conversation, "did not support the Revolution. So Fidel sent the Spanish priests back home." She swept her arm towards Spain. "Cuba will *never again* be told what to do by the so-called first world."

How I admired her fiery resistance, her revolutionary zeal. It was a heady brew. Every cell in my brain was firing. And every other kind of cell in my body was waking up. But so far, my contact with Milagros had been confined to the flirty Spanish lessons. Maybe Aunt Win was right. Milagros was the *Comandante*. I awaited her orders. She seemed to take delight in teasing me with her little glances, touches on my hand, my shoulder, my arm—electric moments, complicit reminders of what we'd shared, just the two of us. But when she went into the kitchen to speak to her mother, the expression on her face changed completely, as if she'd been wearing a façade out on the patio—*la fachada*, they call it. Milagros herself had explained it to me.

"It's a mask, a public face you have to wear to survive in this society."

Now it's masks, I thought. I'm getting in over my head. I'd better watch out.

But it was already way too late.


I spent the mornings exploring the steamy, potholed streets of Santiago. The old city seemed familiar, a sort of tropical St. John's—higgledy-piggledy houses built on steep hills, with a narrow entrance to a landlocked harbour and a Spanish fort where Signal Hill would be. And the people were approachable, opinionated, eager to talk, even pick an argument with a perfect stranger.

"What's this attraction Cubans seem to give off?" I asked Milagros.

She didn't miss a beat. "It's called *chispa*—spark. We Cubans have *chispa*."

"And you know you have it?"

"Oh yes," she said, with one of her glances.

In my wanderings, I'd befriended the newspaper seller by the cathedral, a wizened old man with tiny bright blue eyes and a deep ugly scar on his forearm. One morning, he saw me looking at it.

"From a *machetazo*," he said, "a machete slice. The pain never leaves you. It cuts into your mind."

I sighed. "Sometimes it's hard to control what's in your mind."

He grabbed my arm. "Be careful," he said. "Santiago entrances and bewitches."

It was true. I did feel hijacked, as if some effervescent life force had been injected into my veins. My blood was boiling. Fantasies roared through my mind like hurricanes. I'd picture myself opening the shutter doors to Milagros's bedroom, undressing her, making love to her. I would be husband to Milagros, my Cuban wife, with her glorious, smooth brown body, and stepfather to Vivian, with her almond schoolgirl eyes. So compelled was I by the idea of myself as a Cuban husband, that, God help me, my eyes were constantly welling up with tears of grateful happiness. A glorious end to the loneliness that had been creeping up on me for years and had eventually pushed me out of the priesthood. I'd think of all the ways I could improve Milagros's life—the need to give was becoming confused with my other urges. I even went as far as planning renovations to Rosa and Gabí's house—new pipes, a new kitchen to replace the pre-Revolution fixtures. And on it went.

So far, the subject of need had not come up. At the end of one of our lessons, I broached the topic delicately. "I get the feeling there are shortages. In the street, people keep asking for things—money, chiclets, even soap."

"Pay no attention to them. We call them *jineteros*—jockeys. They ride on the backs of the tourists," Milagros said, with a look of disapproval, almost disgust that so surprised me, I didn't know how to respond.

The priest in me surfaced. "But I can see that people don't have it easy here. All those weary women climbing the hills, hard-faced men sitting idle on park benches. It's a shame."

From the way she lowered her eyes and folded her hands on the table, I should have seen that the subject was taboo. But I couldn't help myself. I moved in close, way closer than I'd ever been. I could smell her hair and see faint spikes of worry lines emanating from the corners of her eyes.

"And how is life for you, Milagros?" I stroked her hand with my clammy fingers.

She pulled away in a flash and her eyes filled with emotion. Anger maybe?

"I have to go to a meeting," she muttered, standing up. "Can't talk today."

She'd cut me—my first machete nick. More hours of sweat and agony on the mattress for me that night. I'd stepped over the boundary, uninvited. I should have known better. I was a CFA— a stupid, ignorant, come-from-away. How could I have any idea of the daily struggle of the Cuban people? The whole escapade was over. I'd made a mess of everything, coming down here with my loneliness in my suitcase.

The next morning, across the sun-flooded patio, I caught a glimpse of Milagros coming out of the shower, brown circles of nipples just visible through her cover-up, curly hair dripping onto her bare shoulders. She called out to me, warm and welcoming as ever.

"Vivian is playing in a concert this afternoon. Would you like to come along?"

At the Music School, the dusty curtain on the little stage was vintage 1960, the instruments were dented and the music scores were yellowing. In the crowded auditorium, I sat next to Milagros, thrilled by the brush against her bare arm and not daring to comment on anything. She's in charge again, I thought.

She gave me a knowing smile. "The school has little material support, but you'll see that when it comes to music, we insist on high standards."

Vivian held her scratched-up flute and performed like a master. Underlying the crystal precision of her playing, I could hear an irresistible, dark velvety rhythm. Shivers ran down my neck. I could barely stop myself from sobbing. After the concert, when we went outside, there was a torrential downpour. I watched the muddy water gushing in rivers down the hills.

"Dear God, I'm flooded."


The next afternoon, I found Milagros on the patio playing the bongos.

"It's Changó's day," she said, "the God of Fire. You must come to our *rumba* tonight."

I went along that night with some trepidation. What was I getting into?

The *rumba* was held in a sweaty little club packed full of people. Everyone stood and watched the drumming and dancing. The dancers wore coloured costumes, each colour representing a Yoruba God. Milagros was in costume too, in flowing white from head to toe.

"I'm the daughter of Obatalà—the God of the Mind," she said, with a seductive look tinged with wisdom, a look I revisit to this day.

The event was attended by people of all ages, mostly Cubans, along with a few elated foreigners, Germans and Italians. At one point, a dancer dressed in the red robes of Changó spun feverishly around a fire and the room took off with excitement. Everyone began to dance. The drumming was authoritative and persistent. The large group of musicians, from the very old to the very young, all bare-chested, kept drumming and drumming, slamming the leather drumheads. As I stood listening, one of the drummers caught my eye. He was a tall, lanky, elderly man with jet black skin and a short crop of curly white hair. As he banged the big conga, his green eyes shone and he looked at me with intent.

I sensed something moving inside me, as if the vibration of the drums was penetrating me, shaking me up, loosening the old calcified bits of myself. At one point, I began to feel a bubble, a trapped piece, traveling up my chest towards my throat. Milagros steered me into the dancing. I watched her body undulating, subtly, deeply. She put her hands on my shoulders, so gently I could barely feel the touch as she moved me to the rhythm.

Almost immediately, the bubble, the trapped piece in my chest, moved up to my throat—I emitted a little noise like a kitten's cry and slow floods of tears started pouring down my cheeks.

"Changó is giving you a *despojo*— a cleansing," said Milagros matter-of-factly.

I stood there with my wet face, having a meltdown in a Santería ceremony. My crying continued as I retreated to the corner. The tears were sweet.

"*Buenas noches*— how are you?"

It was the green-eyed drummer I'd connected with earlier. Feeling expansive as I never had in my life, I shook the man's hand and thanked him for his music. Oozing ease and confidence, laughing what I can only describe as a laugh of pure generosity, he simply took me in his long thin arms and enveloped me in a great warm embrace, leaving a potent scent of lavender cologne on my shirt.

Later, Milagros and I walked back up the hill to the house. The dim streets teemed with people. There was drumming in doorways and in the darkened alcoves. Couples embraced like I had never seen anyone do publicly—or privately, for that matter. I was flushed, urging to grab hold of Milagros. But, still, she felt out of bounds. As we stopped on the corner to look down over the rooftops of the town with its whiffs of smoke from Changó fires, she put her arm in mine.

"So, you've been cleansed," she said, with that same "God-of-the-mind" look, leaving me wondering if I'd seen a tinge of mockery.

As we walked along, she kept her arm in mine, but only loosely. Our skin was touching—but the touch was impersonal, empty. Nonetheless, it was her skin on mine. The lip of a Changó flame was lighting in me. It began to flicker, and by the time we reached the house, it was burning hard. In the jasmine-scented patio, with the Caribbean stars twinkling down on us, Milagros, a glowing beauty in her Obatalá robes, slipped her arm out of mine and lightly brushed a goodnight kiss on my cheek, before I stumbled inside.


Dawn was approaching by the time I found the courage to cross the patio to her room.

I eased open one of the wooden slats in her door and was hit by a strong whiff of lavender cologne. I peered in.

Sitting on the bed was Milagros. In the first light, I could make out the curve of her bare back. Then, next to her, in silhouette, I saw the neat little head of tight curls, the thin shoulders and sinewy, muscled arms of the drummer who had given me the hug of my life at the *rumba*.

I scurried back to my room like a nocturnal creature caught in daylight. I sat on the bed, machetes slicing me. My desire had flamed out, leaving only a few coarse black ashes for me to pick over.

What to do now? Get down on my knees and pray, like the old days? The room looked bare and foreign, full of treachery. I packed my bags.

As the sun made its first searing glint on Santiago harbour, I slipped out the door of Rosa and Gabí's house. In the patio, on the rusty little table, I placed an envelope containing the money to buy a flute for Vivian.

# ACKNOWLEDGEMENTS

Many thanks to all those who helped me create this book: Anne Budgell, Gail Collins, Tom Crothers, Jessica Grant, Ed Kavanagh, Ali Kazimi, Christine Klein-Lataud, Christina Parker, Leslie Vyrenhoek, my Piper's Frith mentors, and to my husband Peter, my sister Elinor, my cousin Helen and all my wonderful friends for their love and support over the years.

Earlier versions of the following stories were published: "Too Unspeakable for Words" in *The Newfoundland Quarterly*, December, 1987. "Fairy-led" in *Canadian Fiction Magazine*, Spring, 1991. "The One I Got" (as "Holy Matrimony") in *The Antigonish Review*, no. 91, 1992. "Learning to Tango" in *The Antigonish Review*, no. 96, 1994. "The Sweetest Meadows" in *The Antigonish Review*, no. 113, 1998. "La Fachada" in *The Antigonish Review*, no. 175, 2013.

Rosalind Gill is a Senior Scholar in French and Translation at Glendon College, York University. She writes fiction and is a literary translator. Her stories and her translations from French and Spanish have appeared in various Canadian journals and magazines. Recently, she has volunteered her translation services to human rights organizations such as Rights Action and PEN Canada.